BROKEN

Book Two in the Forbidden Series

by Melody Anne

COPYRIGHT

© 2014 Melody Anne

All rights reserved. Except for use in any review, the reproduction or utilization of this work in whole or in part in any form by any electronic, mechanical or other means, now known or hereafter invented, including xerography, photocopying and recording, or in any information storage or retrieval system, is forbidden without the written permission of the author.

This is a work of fiction. Names, characters, places and incidents are either the product of the author's imagination or are used fictitiously, and any resemblance to actual persons, living or dead, business establishments, events or locales is entirely coincidental.

Printed and published in the United States of America.

Published by Gossamer Publishing Company

Editing by Alison

DEDICATION

This book is dedicated to Krisi. You make me laugh and inspire me to be a better writer by showing me your real-life romance and how amazing it is. I am so grateful I'm able to know you and have you in my life.

BOOKS BY MELODY ANNE

BILLIONAIRE BACHELORS
*The Billionaire Wins the Game
*The Billionaire's Dance
*The Billionaire Falls
*The Billionaire's Marriage Proposal
*Blackmailing the Billionaire
*Runaway Heiress
*The Billionaire's Final Stand
*Unexpected Treasure
*Hidden Treasure
*Holiday Treasure – **September 2014**

BABY FOR THE BILLIONAIRE
+The Tycoon's Revenge
+The Tycoon's Vacation
+The Tycoon's Proposal

+The Tycoon's Secret
+The Lost Tycoon

RISE OF THE DARK ANGEL

-Midnight Fire – Rise of the Dark Angel – Book One
-Midnight Moon – Rise of the Dark Angel – Book Two
-Midnight Storm – Rise of the Dark Angel – Book Three
-Midnight Eclipse – Rise of the Dark Angel – Book Four – **Coming Soon**

SURRENDER

=Surrender – Book One
=Submit – Book Two
=Seduced – Book Three
=Scorched – Book Four

FORBIDDEN SERIES

+Bound – Book One
+Broken – Book Two – **Coming December 15th**

HEROES SERIES

-Safe in his arms – Novella – *Baby it's Cold Outside* Anthology – Releases **October 28th 2014**
-Her Unexpected Hero – Book One – **Releases Feb 28th 2015**
-Who I am with you – Novella – **Coming soon**
-Her Hometown Hero – Book Two – **Releases June 2015**

PRELUDE

I'M GOING TO peel your clothes away, piece by piece, slowly and completely, and then I'm going to take you hard and fast, leaving you begging me to please you over and over again."

"Why are you doing this to me? Why here?"

"Because I can."

The air weighed down on her lungs, and her entire body pulsed with need. The power, the loss of control, the pure lust shining from his eyes should have disgusted her, should have filled her with fear. But, no matter what she tried, she couldn't resist this man.

When he pinned her against the solid mahogany shelves filled with ancient texts, all she could do was reach for him, desire him, crave him.

CHAPTER ONE

"IT'S TIME, JEWELL."

Slowly turning her head, no color left in her face, Jewell stood with as much grace as possible. The joke of a dress barely covered any of her skin, and it was so tight that what it did hide was hardly hidden at all. But that didn't even matter, did it? All the men sitting out there, waiting, lusting, wanting, preferred it that way.

She was for sale to the highest bidder. And they would do whatever they chose with her. But so what? She was now just an empty shell; all real emotion had been sucked from her. Or at least she hoped it had been.

"You look good. I have no doubt you'll bring in the highest price of the night," Ms. Beaumont told her.

Though the two women had come to an understanding – a friendship of sorts over the last three months, Jewell couldn't think of her as a friend, couldn't think she had any friends. To do what she needed to do in order to survive she had to stand alone.

So Jewell ignored the woman as she stepped in front of the mirror to look at her own image. What she saw was a stranger looking back at her. Her long dark hair had been stripped of its natural color; shimmering platinum tresses now cascaded down her back. This had been her choice, as she'd wanted to erase who she used to be. Expertly applied makeup concealed the circles beneath her eyes, and bright red lipstick matched her low-cut dress to perfection.

Her legs were on full display. Ms. Beaumont, McKenzie, said they were most definitely her best feature — okay, her legs and her back, which was also exposed in all its glory. Jewell refused to meet her employer's gaze in the mirror. If she made eye contact with a single person, she was afraid she would melt down.

Three months she'd been back at Relinquish Control. Three long months. She had lost the case for her brother, and now she was fighting just to get back visitation rights. Even if it wasn't her fault, she'd broken a promise she'd made to her brother. She'd told him she'd be there every weekend, and it had been months since she'd been able to talk to him. He had to believe that she'd abandoned him.

Never.

She was doing all of this for him. If she could save enough money, she'd be able to get him somehow, and the two of them would run away together. The only thing in her life that mattered was little Justin.

"Jewell, it's still not too late to back out of this," Ms. Beaumont said, and her words nearly made Jewell fall apart.

"You know this has to be done," Jewell told her, still refusing to meet her eyes.

"There are other ways," Ms. Beaumont reminded her.

"None of those ways have worked."

Ms. Beaumont, as Jewell had to think of her as, turned away. Jewell was grateful for that.

But Jewell couldn't focus on anything or anyone other than herself. If she focused on anything other than what was in store for her, then she would never get through this auction. She hadn't been with any other men before or since Blake Knight. She hadn't wanted to be with any other men.

She'd tried to block Blake from her mind, but that was an impossibility. Though she'd been with him for only six days, and she hadn't seen him in three months, their relationship had been a perfect storm, constantly leaving her thrashing around in the wind. The fatal moment for her came when he had dropped her back off at the doors to Relinquish Control without even a thought of looking backward.

As soon as she'd decided to work for an escort agency, Jewell had known that her world would never be the same again, but she had suppressed her feelings. Someone mattered more than she did. She would still do anything and everything to have her little brother living with her. The poor boy had to be so frightened right now.

And this was the reason she was now up for auction. Relinquish Control did this once a year, took the girls who were either ready for one last gig or who were interested in doing something a bit more exciting, and paraded them in front of a room full of men, hungry men who were told there were no rules. The clients got to do whatever they wanted with the women they bid the highest price on. Instead of paying for a night or a week, their bid gave them a woman for a full thirty days.

Ms. Beaumont was going to give Jewell half of the proceeds from this night. Half! And from what the other women had said, an escort could sometimes come away with sixty thousand dollars and a treasure trove of jewelry, clothing and other gifts. Surely, if she had at least that much in her bank account, she'd have the power to get her brother back, no matter where he'd been placed.

The money she had made from her first encounter with Blake Knight had all gone to an attorney who had done nothing for her and Justin. She had chosen wrong in who she had paid to represent her. She wouldn't choose so foolishly again, though she still felt lost in how to move forward.

"If you won't change your mind, then it's time," Ms. Beaumont said quietly.

"Let's go." Jewell didn't even recognize her own voice, it was so listless, so monotonic.

Jewell turned from the mirror and followed Ms. Beaumont to the room they'd set up a theater for the event. The audience section was dimly lit, making it difficult for the escorts to see the faces of the men bidding on them, but the lights on the stage shone brightly, ensuring that the bidders didn't miss a single inch of skin. After all, they were there to secure themselves a high-priced whore.

A whore is what they would get.

"Good evening, gentlemen. I am so pleased you have made your way here this evening. All of you have used our services before and know that we guarantee your satisfaction. These women are here for you, and they will love every minute of the time they spend in your... arms." If McKenzie winced slightly when she said that, no one in the audience noticed. "Our...training program is intensive, as you know, and quite costly, and this evening's proceedings allow us to give you only the best. For those who haven't attended one of our auctions before, let me explain how tonight will work."

Ms. Beaumont paused and looked out across the room. The pause heightened the men's anticipation, and they sat there like panting dogs. Jewell took in a deep breath. Some of the girls were actually excited, almost giggly about this event, though they had been trained to hide most of what they felt. Each woman was counting the big bucks she would earn. What did they have to lose? This one job could set them up for an entire year if they were careful with their money. Jewell only hoped the man who picked her wasn't too sadistic.

She *would* be sold tonight. And Jewell had endured some rough nights when she'd been living — not working — on the streets of Seattle, so she could certainly brave a month with a stranger. She just had to keep reminding herself why she was doing it — it was all for Justin.

"You will bid on the girls by holding up your sign. Each bid goes up by increments of five thousand dollars."

The room quieted down as the first girl was brought onstage and made to twist and turn, to show off her assets. She smiled as she tugged on the material of her dress, letting her nipples show. That didn't count as a wardrobe malfunction in this venue. An appreciative murmur rose from the audience, and her price climbed.

Jewell sat with the others off to the side of the stage, where they could see the proceedings, but where the audience couldn't see them. Ms. Beaumont wanted to keep the men waiting, wondering, salivating.

The parading and the bidding and the winning seemed

to go on and on, and Jewell sat stone-still while she waited for her name to be called. She refused to cave in to the tears that were fighting to fall. This wasn't the time or the place. When she had her brother with her, when she was free of this place, free of this life, that was when she could allow herself a few tears.

And not a moment sooner.

"Our next lady is Jewell, and a real gem she is. She's our newest member and has only been with one client to date. Her training is complete, and she is willing and able to make all of your deepest desires come true. Let the bidding begin at twenty thousand."

Signs bobbed in the air as Jewell stood up stiffly and moved onto the stage, turning as she'd been taught, bending down, her body nothing but a tool, an instrument of seduction for profit. The price rose higher and higher, and as no one voiced their bids, she had no clue what type of men were bidding on her, but the higher her price went, the more frightened she became, even though the more money that was spent for her, the more that went into her pocket.

However, men with the kind of money to bid this much expected much more than plain-vanilla missionary-position sex. Her unshed tears now burned inside her, but she pushed them back, made her mind a blank, and turned off all feeling — especially fear. This was just a month — even if it was a very long month. She would get through it.

"Two hundred fifty thousand dollars."

The audience's gasp was loud and clear, and Jewell's body froze. The man had more than tripled the last bid, and he wasn't bothering with holding up a sign. He'd spoken aloud. She had no idea who he was — his voice rang no bells — but she was afraid of him. Would she be able to give what a man willing to pay that price would expect from her?

After tonight she might be of no use to her brother, because the man could do whatever he wanted, and with that kind of money involved, she wasn't sure she'd make it out alive.

CHAPTER TWO

SITTING IN HIS den with the lights turned low, with a pleasant crackling sound coming from the fireplace, and the perfect cognac warming his belly, Blake stared out his window, though he saw nothing but black. It was quite fitting — since blackness was all he'd felt for so long, seeing it was almost soothing.

But a smile turned his lips up, if only a few millimeters, for tonight some of that blackness would fade. It wouldn't disappear — it never would. But tonight he would have Jewell back. Hell, he'd own her outright.

"Sir, I still think this is a very bad idea."

"You dare to argue with me?" Blake thundered.

"You can save the tone for someone who might actually be intimidated by your bark."

The only reason Max Kane was still standing in Blake's den instead of being thrown out onto the street was that the man had worked for him for the past ten years, and he had always been loyal and discreet. And Blake trusted him. That wasn't something that could be said of very many people.

"I'll have her back and she will answer for her lies," Blake said when Max didn't change his stand.

"She told you the truth about her brother. You thought that was a lie," Max pointed out.

"You know what lies she needs to answer for. I will find out what she knows," he said, his eyes narrowing as he raged over the information that had hit him like a freight train three months ago. Then he continued speaking. "And why would she be working as a call girl if she has a brother to care for – a brother she loves so much? There's much she needs to atone for."

"It seems rather obvious to me. Maybe if you asked her the reasons, she would tell you."

"Or maybe she would just lie to me more. Lie by omission. She owes me. I will find out from her, one way or the other."

Max ignored the end of his small speech. "Owes you for what?"

"Do you enjoy pissing me off? I'll focus on the services that I paid for and didn't receive," Blake told him.

"Seriously, Blake? You were the one who dumped her back at the agency before her time was up, so don't try to get away with this crap. I've known you a long time, and though the rest of the world thinks you're a total asshole, I've been privileged enough to see another side of you. Right now, however, you're proving the world right about you." Max's breath came out in an exasperated rush, and he began pacing.

"Good. This is who I am. If you don't like it, you know where the door is," Blake growled.

"It would do you good if I walked out, but you know

I won't," Max said before helping himself to a beer. "It's a wonder I don't drink a lot more working for you," he added with a laugh, and he took a long swallow.

"When did it become okay for you to put down your boss?" Blake asked him.

"Oh, I'm not putting you down, *sir*. I'm only speaking the truth," Max retorted.

Tension hung heavy in the room, and Blake's heart was pounding, his every sense on high alert. The part of the auction that interested him was over. Jewell was soon to be delivered to her new apartment, and then he would see her.

She had no idea who had bid on her, no idea what was coming next. Good. That's what he wanted, to keep her off-kilter. After their last night together, he could still taste the mint in the air, could still hear her gasps of pleasure, could still feel her body tightening around him. He'd tried, but he hadn't been able to keep her from his thoughts. And then he'd found a reason to be with her again.

Finding out that she hadn't been cheating on him, that she really did have a brother, had changed things for him in ways that would surprise a lot of people if they knew the whole story.

"Okay, Max, I can admit that she tried to tell me the truth and I shut her down. But still, Jewell and I have unfinished business. When our business is done, we will both go our separate ways, with us both getting what we truly want," Blake said. "Does that sound more reasonable?"

"I think you're lying to yourself, and I think you're being more than a little irrational. This woman is more than you are making her. Give her a chance and tell her the truth. Don't continue to make her into the whore you have decided she is."

"I don't want to know her. I want her lying beneath me — or on top. I'm an equal-opportunity kind of guy," Blake said with a smirk.

"You could have any woman you want lying in your bed. But it's Jewell you want — that means something."

Blake knew he was being unreasonable, but he wouldn't say that out loud. He wanted Jewell with a passion that he couldn't explain, even knowing what he knew.

"I'll repeat myself," Max continued. "I think there's more between you and Jewell than you're ready to admit, and I won't push you, but I will tell you to be careful. If you're too cruel, you won't stand a chance with her and you won't like how things end."

"If I wanted counseling, I would seek out a professional," Blake replied, and he looked at his watch for the hundredth time.

"Don't worry; I throw in counseling services free of charge," Max said with a grin.

"How about I pay you extra to keep your mouth shut?"

Max laughed. "You could try."

"It doesn't matter. I'll soon grow weary of this woman and then I'll send her on her way — in my own time, and without advice from you or anyone else."

"Who are you trying to convince here, boss? Me? Or just yourself?"

"I don't have to convince anyone," Blake said, "and I don't have to justify myself."

"If that's true, why are you getting so upset?"

"I'm not upset, Max," Blake shouted. In any normal building, the walls would have been shaking visibly.

"Whatever you say, boss. But if you want some real advice, set her free, and then see if she still wants to be with you."

"Set her free? Have you gone bonkers, Max? I just paid quarter of a million dollars for this woman."

"So what? You have more money than any one person could ever possibly spend, and that bid counts as chump change to you. If you want to control her, go ahead and play this out any which way you want, but if you're really interested in this woman, and your other relationships then you're going to have to change your strategy here."

"I'm lost. What are you saying?" Blake followed Max's lead and also began pacing the room. He shouldn't even be listening to this, but he did have a lot of respect for this employee.

"Instead of owning her, offer her a job. Help her do the one thing she has been trying so hard to do," Max said.

"A job?" Blake didn't know what to think of his crazy driver now.

"Yes, a job. You have a lot of places where she could work. Give her a job," Max said slowly.

"But she's already mine."

"For a month," Max pointed out. "Are you so sure you can keep her after that?"

"No. I don't need another employee, and I wouldn't trust her to work for me anyway," Blake insisted.

When there was a long silence, Max found himself wanting to waiver. What if Max had some valid points? No. He didn't, Blake convinced himself before Max spoke again.

"I'm going to get some paperwork done, boss. Let me know when you're ready to leave." Max stood up and walked out of the room.

Blake sat back down, closed his eyes and ran a hand through his hair. He wouldn't need Max tonight. He would get to Jewell's place on his own. He certainly didn't want to see the knowing look on his employee's face again, or to hear those lectures.

Yes, he knew if he told Max enough times to stop doing it, the guy would probably stop. But Max was the voice of reason for Blake when nothing else seemed to make sense. He didn't want to silence the man. Well, maybe he wanted to silence him right now, and at any time when the subject was this woman. But overall, he needed one person he could talk to who wouldn't hold anything back.

Though he'd spent only one week with Jewell, it had been a week that had affected him far more than he cared to admit, even to himself. The woman intrigued him, made him feel things he hadn't ever felt before. But there was no way these feelings could last. He and she just had to play their story out, had to come to a satisfying ending. Once that happened — his hypothetical shrink would call it *closure*, no doubt — Blake would be able to let her go and never think of her again. He needed to let her go in order to do what needed to be done. In order to clear his conscious of what he'd already done.

He hadn't realized quite how great her impact on him had been until he'd started driving away from Relinquish Control three months ago and had seen the door she'd gone through, now closed and fading away in his taillights. The sick feeling in his gut should have made him steer clear of ever seeing her again.

But then Max had come, and then he'd found out what he had found out and his world had been spinning ever since. He shouldn't be doing this, shouldn't be playing with fire. But he was a fool, as so many men were fools, and he had to have answers.

But weren't all men fools? His father sure as hell had been the biggest fool of them all, and his weakness for a woman had cost him his life. Blake wouldn't ever be that weak. It was why he was so determined to purge Jewell from his system, and purge her he would.

Still, there was a piece of him that knew if he were to throw her away it would ruin all his chances of making other relationships. But, he didn't believe the stories she had told him. She was as cold as him, and he would prove that.

Or maybe both of them were just fated for damnation. He would soon find out.

CHAPTER THREE

THE WORLD SEEMED to be rushing by in a blur. While the auction continued for the other girls, Jewell was rushed off the stage as soon as she was "won." She saw none of the money exchanging hands; she just felt her coat being placed on her shoulders, and then was led out the back door to a waiting car.

"Where am I going? Who bought me?" she asked the alarmingly large man holding open the back door.

"I'm not at liberty to say," he told her in a deep voice that was as terrifying as his size was. "Please get into the vehicle."

He'd said *please*, but it was obvious his words weren't a polite request. She had been paid for, and his boss, whoever he might be, wanted his merchandise *now*. Those long-threatening tears pressed even closer, and the burning grew more acute. But Jewell still fought to keep her outward composure.

She could try to run. Although she probably wouldn't get far on the impractical heels she was wearing, she could make a valiant effort. You never know. But then where would she be? She wouldn't have money or a place to live, and she would be no closer to getting custody of her poor brother, a sensitive, grieving ten-year-old who was most likely stuck in a foster family from hell.

Yes, she could die. This man who had bought her could be a ruling sheik from a foreign land who planned to enslave her, but wasn't she already enslaved? Even if the chances of her getting out of this debacle unhurt were slim to none, at least she had a sliver of hope. And think how much had been bid for her! The fifty percent she'd get when the gig ended meant her beloved Justin would finally be hers.

That was the hope she held on to. That was the reason she finally climbed into the back of the car — an experience eerily like the first time she'd left the agency, when she'd been taken to Blake. She couldn't help but think of the man as the car revved up and headed away from Relinquish Control.

Her biggest hope for the next month — and it couldn't be very big — was to find that the man who bid on her was like Blake. When she'd first met him, she wouldn't have believed that she'd ever hope such a thing. But the week with him had changed her. Though he'd pushed her with his demands, and though he'd made her do things far from her comfort zone, he'd also made her go up in flames, made her desperate for more. She very much doubted she'd be so lucky with her new master, or whatever the hell she was supposed to call him. The feelings she'd had with Blake, and men who inspired them, were surely rare.

Jewell leaned back in the plush leather seat and struggled to clear her head. This was all beyond her control, so what good would it do to worry herself any more than she already had? Whatever happened would happen, and she wasn't going to let herself lament a fate when she didn't know yet what it would be.

When the car stopped and her door opened, Jewell just looked up at the massive suit-covered chest of the man waiting for her step from the car. Her nerves were in such a state that her stomach wanted to heave, but there was nothing in her stomach anyway — she'd been unable to eat — so what good would it do her?

So she finally climbed out and stood there on shaky legs as the driver shut the door. What on earth was she supposed to do next? She half suspected that the man was enjoying the tension of the moment and had decided to draw it out to torment her.

"Here's your key. Your apartment is on the fifth floor, unit 512. Have a nice evening." With that, he walked around to the front of the car, got back inside and drove away.

Jewell wasn't sure how long she stood on the street watching the taillights disappear, but when her feet began screaming — these nosebleed heels were killing her — and the evening chill started seeping through her thin jacket, she turned and looked at the front of the apartment building.

A doorman stood silently next to an elaborate double door, his attention on her as he waited to see what she was going to do. Was this a joke? How did the man who'd purchased her know that she wouldn't run?

That was a stupid question. The bidder knew she wouldn't run, because if she did, she wouldn't be paid. And he'd get a full refund anyway, so he could buy a new woman to slake his lust. Of course she was going to go inside; of course she was going to see what fate had in store for her.

With her head held as high as she could hold it, she approached the intimidating building.

"Good evening, Ms. Weston," the attendant said as he held the door open.

That stopped her, and she stared at him in surprise. "How do you know who I am?" As soon as the words came out, she once again felt unutterably foolish.

"Your driver informed me that he would be bringing you by at this time," the man replied in a professionally polite tone.

"Oh… That makes sense…" Jewell paused for a moment. "What's your name?" The longer she delayed, the longer she could pretend she wasn't a victim on the way to the sacrificial altar.

"My name is Flynn," he said with what seemed to be a genuine smile.

"It's very nice to meet you, Flynn. You can call me Jewell." If she were going to be here for a while, she would probably grow to like the fellow.

"It's nice to meet you, too," he said, still holding open the door.

When she didn't move, he added, "Can I help you with anything else?"

"I…um…haven't been here before," she told him. Though she knew where she was supposed to go — unit 512 — she wasn't sure how to get to the apartment from where she was now. She was embarrassed to admit that to him, because now he was sure to know exactly what she was and why she was there — to be someone's lady of the night — and of the day, too.

"That's no problem, Ms. Weston. The key you have in your hand will give you access to the elevator over there to your right. Once you're inside, insert the key in the slot and push your floor number," he told her, his expression unchanging.

"Thank you, Flynn," she said, and she finally walked inside, her eyes widening at the building's luxurious lobby.

A security desk stood tall against the back wall; a man behind it was looking at monitors. Real live plants flanked a sitting area where comfortable tan leather chairs, currently empty, sat in a circle. The gray marble floors were freshly polished and shining, and the tall windows would bathe the room in light while the sun reigned in the sky.

Once she'd made it to the elevator, Jewell pushed the Up button, then had to wait only a few seconds before the doors opened and she was inside. Finding the slot for her key was easy. The doors shut and she was riding smoothly up to the fifth floor.

She arrived before she was ready and almost didn't step off before the doors closed again. Her knees shaking even more than before, Jewell crept down the wide carpeted hallway until she found the door to her apartment. She had no idea how long she'd been standing there when she realized that the key in her hand was nearly cutting her skin open. She had the damned key in a death grip.

"It's now or never. No matter how long you stand here, you'll eventually have to see what's on the other side of that door," Jewell told herself just beneath her breath.

When she slipped the key into the lock, the door slid open easily, and she forced herself to walk inside. The entryway was large and well lit, and after shutting the door behind her, she stopped and listened for any sounds from within.

"Hello?" she called out, and then waited. No answer.

Could it be possible that no one was there with her? Why would someone spend *two hundred and fifty thousand dollars* and then not collect what was owed to him? It made no sense.

Her heart thundering, she slowly made her way deeper into the apartment, her stiletto heels clicking on the marble beneath her feet. The entry opened up into a large living room, completely furnished but lacking any personal touches.

Beiges and soft greens seemed to be the theme of the apartment. If she could decorate any way she wanted, it wouldn't be what she'd choose, but she'd also never be able to afford a place this luxurious, and she wouldn't complain about staying there. Well, she wouldn't complain until she had to find out what the price — the *barter* price — was for her room and board.

"Hello?" she called out once more, but again only silence answered her.

She found a fully appointed kitchen, the stainless-steel fridge full of soda, juice, and perishables, the cupboards stocked, the newest and best small appliances sitting atop granite counters. An intimate table sat in the dining room, the welcoming seats of the chairs covered with a light green fabric.

She saw a hallway and went down it, sure that it led toward the bedrooms, and instead encountered a set of open double doors with a soft light coming from the room behind them. Stepping inside, she froze.

She'd called out twice with no answer. But she now knew she wasn't alone.

The figure took its time turning toward her, and the color drained completely from Jewell's face. She'd almost have preferred some sadistic sheik to the man now facing her, his eyes hard and unreadable, his muscles tight. He looked ready to pounce, and her throat closed with nervous tension.

"Good evening, Jewell. We meet again."

CHAPTER FOUR

SHOCK…FEAR…RELIEF…

Why was she feeling relief? No. She didn't want to be with Blake Knight. Just the sound of his voice slamming into her already fractured nerves had left her barely able to stand. She'd been with the man for a week, just a week, the last time around, and she had barely survived the ups and downs.

And now her sentence with him lasted for a month. Why had he bid on her? Why did he want her again when he'd dumped her so coldly and with such finality? He'd told her she was a liar, that he never wanted to see her again. Why would he have paid a quarter of a million dollars to take her back when he'd been the one to return her — as if she'd been defective?

Yet here he was, standing before her in all his dark glory, his custom suit molded to his shoulders, his gray eyes boring into hers, his very presence overwhelming her, making her knees knock together.

Jewell finally managed to tear her gaze from his, and

she looked around the room, a room that he seemed so out of place in. For a mere mortal like her, this place was elegant as sin, but the Blake Knights of the world lived on a far higher level.

Still, she had no chance of forgetting he was there. Without moving a muscle or saying a word, he commanded a room — commanded her — though she hoped to the highest reaches of heaven that he wasn't aware of that fact. The man was so raw, so powerful. His presence seemed to suck all the air from the room.

When he took a step toward her, Jewell found herself riveted to the floor. Yet every instinct inside her told her to run, told her that retreat was her only option. She'd thought she'd seen the last of him. No matter how much she had tried to prepare herself for the new person who would be entering her life, she couldn't have ever been prepared for it to be Blake.

Her heart thudding violently, she watched his slow but deliberate approach and wondered whether she would pass out. It wouldn't be surprising if she did; after all, she couldn't breathe.

When his eyes caressed her body from the tips of her toes to what seemed like every last strand of her hair, a shudder passed through her. She was his property and he was assessing the merchandise, and though his expression should have frozen her, it did the impossible and heated her to her very core.

"Why?" She couldn't seem to get any other words past her closed throat.

His lips turned up in the tiniest of smiles as he invaded her personal space, seeming to drain her very essence from her as he lifted a hand and ran a finger along her cheekbone. Looking into Blake's eyes became way too much for her, and she briefly closed her own as she took a breath and tried to gain some semblance of strength.

"May I offer you each something to drink?"

It took a moment for Jewell to realize that someone else had entered the room. Opening her eyes, she turned to find an attractive woman in her early thirties at most, with a neutral expression on her face.

"I…Where did you come from?" Jewell asked. She'd called out twice with no answer. And yet Blake and some strange woman had both been there.

"She was told to wait in back," Blake said with a smile. Of course the woman would be at his command, whoever she was. Everyone was at Blake's command. Jewell – hell, the rest of the world, were simply there to do his bidding, or so he thought.

"No. You're dismissed for the evening, Elsa," Blake then said.

Jewell watched as the woman disappeared.

"Blake, I don't understand this," Jewell said, the shock beginning to wear off as agitation took its place. "I'm in a strange place with some woman mysteriously popping in, and you…and…I don't understand," she finished quietly, twisting her fingers together.

"Sit down, Jewell."

She waited a moment for him to continue, and when he didn't, she looked around. Should she obey like the puppet she was supposed to be? She just didn't know.

"Unless you'd rather walk straight into the bedroom," he added.

There was no mistaking the desire that was burning in his eyes. Though this sitting room was new and strange to her, Jewell thought it a safer zone than the room Blake had proposed. So she moved backward, somehow found a chair, and fell into it.

"I don't know why you came back for me. I don't know why you paid so much money for me when it was you who dumped me back off at the agency. None of this makes sense, Blake. This isn't what you want — not really. This has to be about power…or revenge…or something I can't even fathom."

He walked up to her and leaned down, caging her against her chair, making the breath she'd finally taken rush back out of her tight throat.

She couldn't read the look in his eyes, couldn't figure out what was going on inside his head, but she knew that, no matter what he was thinking, it couldn't be good. A man who had shelled out so much for a woman would certainly get his money's worth — one way or another.

"We have things to discuss, Jewel. The two of us began a journey three months ago, a journey that we haven't yet come close to finishing," he said, his tone smooth, his eyes on fire.

"Our journey is long over, Blake," she said, her voice barely above a whisper.

"That's where you're so very wrong, Jewell. I'm not done with you yet," he said, leaning down farther and letting his breath wash over her burning skin.

"No…," she said, her body quaking.

"Oh, yes, Jewell. We are only just now beginning."

CHAPTER FIVE

JEWELL CLOSED HER eyes and tried to think, tried to get her head around what was happening. "You don't want me," she told him, not sure if she was trying to convince herself or trying to convince Blake. "You know you don't."

"Yes, I want you, Jewell. Just as much as you want me. I discovered some facts after you were gone," he began when he paused.

She couldn't help but correct him. "You mean after you screwed me on your truck and then dumped me off like the trashy whore I am, at the back door of Relinquish Control."

He laughed, actually laughed at her words, making her want desperately to reach out and slap the smug look right off his face. How dare he laugh at her? He was in serious danger right then, and from the continued mirth she saw dancing in his eyes, it was apparent that he knew that — and wasn't in the least worried.

"Calm down, Jewell. We're not getting anywhere with

your little burst of temper. Though, I must say, it turns me on to see such fire light up in your eyes," he said with a wink. "But we can certainly put your heightened emotions to better uses than venting."

Oh how she wished she could be as cold and unaffected as this ice sculpture of a man. He wouldn't know true human emotion if it were right in front of him — which it was, since she was aching inside and out.

"Why are you the way you are, Blake? How can you be so cavalier, so unfeeling? Don't you care at all that you make me lose any sense of control?" She was vulnerable, angry, and struggling with other emotions she didn't even know how to name.

"I see nothing wrong with the way I act," he said levelly, refusing to back away despite her words. As a matter of fact, he drew nearer, and there wasn't much nearer to go. "I like who I am, and no one can *make* you feel any emotion, Jewell. We choose how we feel; we choose what we think, what we want, what we desire. You can choose to enjoy this, or you can choose to run from it, but either way, you are mine, and I know you want me. I know you want *all* of this. To try to escape when we've come so far together would be foolish."

The way his breath whispered over her flesh, across her cheek, her lips, her neck, made her shudder. She had no doubt there was fire burning in her eyes, flames hot enough to match the embers burning in his. To even try to deny it would be a wasted effort — they'd both know she was lying.

Jewell instead did something she knew she'd later regret — or maybe not — but she acted with emotion, with rage, with desire. She clenched her fist involuntarily and watched, almost as an outsider looking in, as her fist rose and slammed into the side of his face.

And yet his expression remained neutral, and though he flinched, it was almost imperceptible. He simply stared at her with eyes that were still cold, still all-knowing and hyperaware. That was outside of enough. And then she was pulling back and slamming her fist into his jaw again.

When she still didn't get a reaction from him, she lost all vestiges of sanity, and lifted both hands, her claws coming out as she reached for him and tugged on his hair. She was beyond reason and control now, lost in a blaze of fury. The past few months had come to a head.

Who in the hell did he think he was? It wasn't fair that that he could mess so easily with her emotions and what she was feeling, and that he even got to choose her destiny. He had no right to make her feel anything. She'd thought she could spend the next month as a hollow shell, devoid of any feeling, whether good or bad, but how could she possibly be like that with Blake? She knew this was a battle she couldn't win.

But for some reason she couldn't stop herself, couldn't retreat, which meant she could only keep fighting.

"I hate you!" she screamed when he still showed her no emotion.

Then, so quickly that she had zero chance of stopping him, he thrust out one hand and grabbed both of hers, then jerked her arms up while the fingers of his other hand snaked behind her head and tangled in her hair.

Before she even thought of struggling, she was being pulled up from the chair and shoved backward until she was flat against the wall, his body a mass of steel boxing her in. Her arms were stretched high above her head, her heart thudding, her breath gone yet again.

Blake displayed just a hint of emotion as he pushed against her, and she couldn't mistake how hard their struggle had made him. Somehow, that turned her rage into a burning passion — a passion she despised herself for feeling.

Before she was able to recover herself, to firmly lock away anything other than hatred for the man now entrapping her, his eyes narrowed and he went on the attack. He quickly bent his head down and captured her mouth in a kiss of pure — and impure — possession.

And the three months they'd been apart evaporated in an instant and she was right back with him, right where they'd been their last night together, where anger and frustration had morphed into heat and passion.

His kiss was masterful, and it didn't take him long to part her closed lips and access the warm recesses of her needy mouth. There was hunger, danger, and so much more in the way he held her body, the way he completely devoured her, leaving no room for thoughts of anything or anyone but him.

One feeling merged into the next as he plundered her mouth, intimately reacquainting himself with the feel and touch of her, making her knees grow weak, her heart beat erratically, and her core heat to the point of boiling. This was pure sex at its most basic level.

His fingers tightened in her hair and he moved his body rhythmically against hers, his arousal pressing as intimately against her womanhood as their clothes would allow. She was ready, so ready, for him to take her.

"I want you, Jewell; I want you more than I've ever wanted any other woman. You make me burn," he said when he pulled back for air. He trailed his lips down her throat after his words made her insides seem to dissolve.

Jewell tried to remember why this was wrong. She tried to regain her equilibrium, but she couldn't think, couldn't move, couldn't even breathe, let alone try to resist this pull he had on her. Even knowing she would hate him and herself even more than she already did, she couldn't stop herself from responding.

The only way this would end was if he put on the brakes.

But Blake obviously wasn't finished yet. He freed her hands only to let his fingers glide down her body, stroking the sensitive flesh of her sides, hips and ass. Her head fell back and a sigh escaped her lips while his mouth caressed the skin of her neck.

It took a moment for her to realize he had finally stilled. He rested his hands on her hips, and his mouth no longer made its seductive way along her skin. She slowly tilted her head forward and once again found her eyes captured by his ardent gaze.

It must have been an eternity that the two of them stood there, neither saying a word, their breathing now returning to something like normal — though Jewell's body would never be normal again. She didn't know what to do or say, and still couldn't think with his hard body pressed against hers.

But the silence was getting to her, and when she thought she couldn't take it another second longer, she finally opened her lips, ran her tongue slowly along their swollen edges, and then took a deep breath before she spoke.

"That didn't prove anything" was what came out, but

not nearly as strongly as she'd intended.

Blake threw her a hint of a smile and leaned a little closer. When he finally replied, his mouth was back to within inches of hers.

"I think it proved exactly what it was supposed to, Jewell."

"And what is that, Blake? That you have power over me, that no matter what I do or say, you'll still get exactly what you want? Well, if that's what you're trying to prove, congratulations, you did it. Yes, you can force me to do what you want. You're bigger, stronger, and far more manipulative than I am. And anyway, this is what you paid for, right?" She hoped she'd infused her voice with as much disdain as she possibly could.

"You've developed some bite in the time we've been apart," he said, his voice smooth and sounding almost… impressed.

She wasn't sure she liked that. She was trying to sound fierce, intimidating, frightening. She wasn't supposed to be turning him on more than he already was.

"Yes, I have. In the months since you so carelessly discarded me, I've developed a bit of a spine. You'll find that I'm not the same submissive little girl you abused to your heart's desire. So, you see, you've wasted your money, Blake Knight, because I won't be what you want."

"Oh, Jewell, I know exactly what I want," he said, running his hand through her hair again. "And it most certainly is you. Besides, wasn't I promised *anything* I want for the next thirty days?"

A shudder ran through her. She needed the money this month would bring in, and they both knew it. But she hadn't counted on how much she loathed the idea of being some man's toy, any man's toy. But Blake's especially, because she knew she wouldn't be able to keep her emotions out of it.

"You did buy me, so, yes, I guess you get to do whatever you want. But I won't enjoy it; nor will I try to make it better for you. Be warned."

"That's where we'll agree to disagree," he whispered. "I know for a fact that not only will you enjoy it, but you'll beg me for more. And more. And more." With those last six words, he brushed his lips against hers. "And I'll definitely give it to you."

What he said made liquid heat course through her veins. Yes, he'd given her pleasure, pleasure beyond anything she could ever imagine existed. But he'd also given her so much pain. And the pain was what she was afraid of. She'd suffered enough emotional trauma to last her a lifetime.

He could so easily destroy her — she had no doubt of that. But he owned her, at least her body, and there was nothing she could do about it. Why fight it? Why even try? Because he could own her body, but he couldn't own her mind, her heart, her soul, or at least what pieces of those things she still had.

"You know I'll hate you forever, Mr. Knight." *Knight!* Pschaw! No shining armor here.

Only a tiny spark igniting in his eyes showed her that her words had registered. When his lips parted, she waited for the backlash. She didn't get it.

"I don't require any emotion from you except for passion," he said almost dismissively. "A nice, basic animal response."

The words stung more than she'd ever admit.

"Then we're on the same page," she told him, "because you won't get anything other than my body." How desperately she wished that he would give her just a bit of breathing room.

"Ah, Jewell, the fire in you is what made me come back, what made me have to see this through to the end. What made me know that I can get whatever I want out of you."

"How long will it be until the end? Will I really be free of you after thirty days?"

She waited as he stared her down in silence, showing nothing in his ice-cold eyes. She wouldn't break the silence, though. This was up to him.

"No, Jewell. We won't be done until I'm finished with you."

Jewell had no idea what that could possibly mean.

CHAPTER SIX

THE EXCRUCIATING EMOTIONS holding sway over Jewell's fragile frame continued their chaotic dance in her veins as Blake finally stepped back. Then, almost on a dime, Blake broke into a smile. "Follow me, Jewell. I'm going to the kitchen."

Without waiting to see if she would obey or not, he pivoted on his heel and walked from the room, leaving her to sag against the wall as she prayed her knees wouldn't give out on her. Less than thirty minutes in Blake's presence and she was a complete mess. She'd been in better shape when she'd been worried she might have been sold to some sadistic stranger. But then again, Blake was no stranger to sadism.

She kept her distance, though, but not because she was afraid that he'd hurt her physically. Maybe it was because she knew what would happen if she ended up in his arms again — she wouldn't be able to deny to herself how very much she was attracted to this despicable man, and that mortified her. She should be heading for the hills and screaming all the way. But she was still here.

When she finally stepped into the kitchen, he was making a pot of coffee, which seemed to irritate her more than anything else he'd done in the last half hour. Why? She had no idea. Maybe it was because he felt he could do whatever he chose to do whenever he chose to do it. And he did have that right, at least with her.

Power. Blake Knight had that in spades. Some people were born with it, and some were destined to wield it.

Though the apartment was light, airy even, to have Blake standing in her new roomy kitchen made the place seem to shrink, to instantly grow dark. This was his domain and she was his paid mistress, and she felt it in every bone — no, in every *cell* — of her body.

When the coffee was ready, Blake poured them each a cup and, without a word, led Jewell back to the sitting room they'd been in before. He made himself comfortable, and she bet he was enjoying watching how *un*comfortable she was. She felt like a puppet when she obediently followed him from room to room, waiting to see what was coming next.

With her legs trembling badly, she decided it best if she just sat down on the nearest couch and focused on her coffee. No matter how long he dragged this out, she'd find out his next move fairly soon. And why worry about anything? In this game, he was fated to be the only winner.

"You seem very ungrateful, Jewell."

"Do you honestly think I'm about to thank you for buying me?" To her complete shock, she realized that she'd been screeching at him just now. What sort of a human being was she becoming? Did she even deserve to get her little brother back if she had so little control over herself?

"I expected a little bit of appreciation. Anyone could have paid for you, and they wouldn't be nearly as… acquainted with your desires."

"You amaze me, Blake…"

He quickly interrupted. "Thank you, Jewell."

"That wasn't meant as a compliment," she told him.

"But I'll take it as one," he replied. "I know what you like and I know you aren't unhappy to be here."

"Then you don't know anything." She tried to keep emotion out of her voice, but it was beyond her powers.

"Would you like for me to take you back to the agency? I'm sure there are other men there who would love to have you for a month…or longer."

She couldn't tell what he was thinking or feeling. His cold eyes held hers captive, but they didn't reveal a single thought contained in his head. Should she say yes and take her chances on someone else? She chose to say nothing.

"I didn't think so, Jewell. You may be fighting this, but you aren't disappointed that I'm the one who won you."

"That's exactly what this is, Blake. A contest. I'm a prize in a game I never wanted to play," she said, struggling to suppress her tears of frustration.

"You're the one who chose to be employed at Relinquish Control."

Her shoulders sagged. "I had no choice," she whispered.

"There's always a choice, Jewell," he countered. He seemed angry with her for working there, but that made no sense. And he had been a customer there, so how did it make him any better than her? She barely refrained from asking him that.

"*Of course there is.* You're right, as always. So why don't we quit dancing around this and you just tell me what you expect from me?"

His expression didn't change as he looked at her for several long moments. She'd thought billionaires were always on the go because time equaled money, but he didn't seem to have any problem at all drawing this out.

"What do you think I want, Jewell?"

"To prove your power. You couldn't control me, so you're back for another chance to put the win in your column." She hoped to see something in his eyes this time. But she didn't.

"If that were what I wanted, I could have it right this instant. This is just the beginning, but the ending isn't in doubt here, because you want me as much as I want you. If I felt in the mood to play power games, I'd do it in the boardroom. The way things play out there is less predicable, though even there I always win."

She gasped. "Damn, you're arrogant."

"It's not arrogance when it's true."

She didn't know what to say to that. There was no arguing with him. "Just get this over with, Blake. I've had a long day — a long year, for that matter — and the sooner this song and dance ends, the sooner I can get some rest."

And she was telling it like it was — all of a sudden, she felt exhaustion threaten to pull her under. She had run the gamut of emotions over the last few months, and especially today, and she found herself barely able to stay awake now, much less agile enough to spar verbally with this man.

When Blake stood and moved over to sit by her, she didn't try to object. At least he was finally going to *really* speak to her, finally going to map out what was to come.

"It doesn't matter, you know," she said, her defenses

down.

"What doesn't matter?" he asked while reaching for her hand, which she allowed him to take.

When he rested their joined fingers on his leg, she felt a spark, but she repressed it as far as she could.

"Anything. What I feel, what I want. None of it matters," she told him.

"I don't agree with that, Jewell. What you want is very important." That contradicted everything he had been saying to her, everything he was doing. She couldn't keep up with him.

When he pulled her onto his lap and drew her head against his chest, she knew she should resist him, but she couldn't. This man was causing her so much pain, but he also seemed to be shouldering some of that pain by as simple an act as wrapping her in his arms. It made no sense, but what in her world made sense any more? Since the death of her mother, she'd felt like a passenger on a roller coaster without brakes, and all she could do was pray that at some point the ride would manage to stop, and she would end up safely back on solid ground.

"How long will this go on? Do you want me broken? If that's the case, it's close to happening," she told him, knowing she would regret the words later, when she felt stronger. *If* she ever felt stronger…

"I don't ever want to break you, Jewell," he said, letting his fingers sift through her hair.

"I thought that's what you loved to do, Blake — break women."

"I won't deny that doing that has brought me pleasure in the past. But can't a person change?"

"No. Not like that. I don't think someone can change

that much and that quickly. Especially if they don't want to."

"It's very simple, Jewell. I have decided I don't want to let you go, not until I get the answers I am searching for," he said and she felt again like she couldn't breathe.

What answers? She was too tired to even try to begin to figure out these riddles he was speaking of. She fought to free herself from his arms, but they were like vises. The more she struggled, the more they tightened around her. She finally gave up. It was all too clear how useless her struggles were.

"And what if I don't go along with your plan?"

"I have something you want, so I think you will." His voice was filled with the utmost confidence.

"There is nothing you could have that would make me want to stay with you," she said, her voice stronger now.

"You don't know what I have, Jewell."

She didn't want to ask him, didn't want to know what he was holding over her, but she knew this night wouldn't end until he got to make his point. So, though well aware she wouldn't like whatever he had to say, she opened her mouth and let the words come out.

"What is it, Blake? What do you know? What do you have?"

Her heart pounded during the long moments of silence that followed. Blake spoke at last.

"I have access to your brother."

CHAPTER SEVEN

A FEW MINUTES might have passed, perhaps an hour. Jewell didn't know, because after Blake spoke of her brother, her heart had stopped and her breath had lodged in her throat.

"But you didn't believe me about my brother," she finally managed to say.

"I didn't," he admitted.

"What's going on, then?" she asked. "I'm lost, Blake."

"Let's just say that I did a little bit of research, Jewell. I have found out quite a lot."

"Why are you doing this to me? This is your idea of a cruel joke, isn't it? Do you find my pain amusing? Hell, that's a stupid question. You're all about causing pain." He finally released her and she jumped up and began pacing as she waited for him to respond.

He stood up slowly and approached her with measured strides, intimidating in his muscularity, his massiveness. She backed away but soon found herself once again against the wall with Blake blocking her in, trapping her.

"I don't joke around," he said, his words low and ringing with the sound of truth.

"But…"

"I discovered you weren't deceiving me, and I found out everything about your brother. As I told you, I have access to your brother."

"I'll ask again, Blake. How? And what is the price you want from me? And what does that mean?"

"Does it make any difference?"

His words were a clear challenge, and all the fight left her. "No." And it didn't make a difference. She would do anything to see Justin. Hadn't she already proved it the minute she'd agreed to work for Relinquish Control?

He rested his fingers against her hip. "Are you going to continue to fight me?" he asked her.

"Yes." She was surprised when the word came from her throat. Why would she risk this?

She wouldn't. Before she could correct herself, he leaned against her and brushed her mouth with his.

"I wouldn't have it any other way," he said, his words vibrating against her lips.

"I didn't mean that. I will do whatever it takes to get my brother."

"I didn't say I would give him to you. I said I have access to him," he pointed out.

"What in the hell does that mean?"

"I want answers, Jewell."

"What answers?" she snapped. There was a long pause before he spoke again.

"You will find out," he told her. Again, more riddles.

"Fine, Blake. You win. You can have what you want," she said, though everything in her fought against even saying those words.

"Don't become boring, Jewell." He pressed his thickness against her. "Don't make it too easy to figure you out."

"I don't think that's something you'll ever have to worry about, Blake, because I can't even figure myself out, let alone allow you to figure me out. None of this is right, and none of it is predictable, but I guarantee you that no matter what you do, you will never own me completely." She shouldn't continue fighting him, but it was almost as if another person were speaking.

"That's where you're wrong, Jewell, very wrong. I won't settle for less than all of you."

Her body felt molten. Even though she didn't want to want him, even though she knew he was a monster, she also knew how good it felt to lie in his arms. She wanted him and she hated him for it.

"You'll be very disappointed, then, Blake. But you're a man of your word. You have clearly paid for the rights to my body. And because I know you do have the power to access Justin, you have bought my obedience. But having my body and even having me desire you doesn't mean that I've agreed to give you any other part of me."

"I can have anything I want, Jewell."

"Not quite, Blake. You can have anything that money can buy."

"It bought you," he pointed out.

"Actually, you just *rented* me, and not all of me at that. I hope you know that I find you despicable, and that I do indeed hate you."

His eyes flashed at the words and the tone she used, and she waited for her punishment. She had to learn not to respond when he goaded her, or her time with him would be unbearable, because no matter what she could possibly do to him, he could do it to her ten times as painfully without breaking a sweat.

"If I believed that, we would have a problem."

He reached into her hair and tugged it hard, then crushed his lips against hers. She fought him for a moment before all thoughts evaporated from her mind. This was the power he had. No matter how angry he made her, a few seconds in his arms and she was fully under his spell.

When she'd submitted to him totally, that's when he released her. She slowly opened her eyes and saw unmitigated triumph in his expression, and once the fog cleared from her muddled brain, she stiffened.

Okay, this wasn't working. She'd known that he'd always win in a power struggle, but her emotions kept getting in the way. She needed to go a different route dealing with Blake. But simply to answer him right now required her to pretend to possess an unconcern she didn't at all feel. And yet she barreled ahead.

"I hope you don't take my passion as anything more than my body responding, Blake. I can despise you and still desire you. After all, you were a pretty good lay."

He let her go and turned his back to her, leaving her to lean back against the wall and hope her legs wouldn't fail her.

After a few heartbeats, he swung back around and smiled at her, giving her no idea what he was thinking about.

"You'll eventually learn more about me, Jewell, about what 'makes me tick.' We obviously haven't spent enough time together if you really think I'm so easily discouraged. But that's okay — we have all the time in the world to get to know each other."

"We have thirty days," she countered. "And what about my brother? Do I have to please you before I get to take him home?" It took everything inside her to say the words without scorn.

Blake moved back to the couch and sat down as if he had no other place in the world to be.

"Don't worry about it. In the end, you will see your brother. That's what you want, isn't it, Jewell?"

"Of course that's what I want," she growled. After finally pushing away from the wall, she went in for another round of pacing.

"And you have proved that you will do whatever it takes to make that happen."

She didn't trust the calm she heard in his voice, the way he said those words. It didn't take a genius to see that this was simply the eye of the storm. What she couldn't figure out was what was in this for him. "What do you get out of this, Blake?" she finally asked.

The smile that turned up his lips was her first sign that she wasn't going to like his next words any more than she'd liked anything he'd had to say so far. In fact, she'd probably like it less. The confidence emanating from him made that sick feeling in her stomach even stronger.

"We've gone over this ground before. I get anything I want, don't I, Jewell." It wasn't a question. It was a statement — and one he had no doubt was completely factual.

"No, Blake. No one gets everything they want," she told him. "I'm not making an argument. I'm simply telling you the truth."

He just threw her another smile, one making it clear

that her words hadn't put him out one bit. It seemed that nothing she could do or say would throw him off the high horse he always rode. When he stood up, she waited for his next assault, but instead of coming toward her, he was heading away.

"What are you doing now?" she asked when he looked to be exiting the room.

"I'm done for the night. We'll discuss this more tomorrow," he said, and he kept on walking.

Before she was able to say another word, she heard the front door open and close. He'd left. With shaking knees, she proceeded down her hallway, found what had to be her bedroom, and sagged onto the bed, not bothering to change, not bothering to open her eyes again once they drifted shut.

Blake Knight had reappeared in her life with a hurricane-like force, disrupting everything in his path. But he wasn't going to grow weaker as he continued on his journey, much less calmly drift back out to wherever he came from. No. That wasn't his style. He would return again and again until he got what he wanted.

For now, that appeared to be her. And there was nothing she could possibly do to stop him.

CHAPTER EIGHT

JEWELL LOOKED FUZZILY at the clock near her head. Six in the morning, it said, and, oddly enough, she wasn't tempted to throw it against the wall. She'd finally slept, and it had done her good. Instead of feeling defeated, she jumped out of bed and almost danced into her large new en-suite bathroom. She even added an extra little wiggle in her hips. When she'd been at Blake's place three months ago, he had installed video cameras everywhere to monitor her actions. He might or might not have done the same thing here, but she just didn't care. If he wanted a show, a show he would get.

When she'd last looked in the mirror, she'd felt hollow, drained. But not now. Today, she had a purpose. Blake might think he owned her, and in a way he did, but in the end she and Justin would be reunited and the two of them would run to the farthest reaches of the planet. No one would be able to separate them again.

After finding the walk-in closet crammed with clothing — a whole new wardrobe — Jewell dressed and put on makeup, then stood before the full-length mirror and smiled. As she stepped into her kitchen, the telephone rang.

Jewell couldn't remember the last time someone had rang her. Wait. Yes, she could. It had been Blake. She was sure it was him now. She should ignore it, but what good would that do her?

"Hello," she answered.

"Jewell?"

"Ms. Beaumont?" Jewell replied, sure it was her boss.

"Yes, it's me. I shouldn't be doing this, but I have set up a consultation for you with a very good attorney. I don't want to get your hopes up, but I promised to help you and this is my way of doing so," she said quickly.

"I...uh...didn't expect this," Jewell replied. Yes, she and McKenzie had spoken a lot over the last couple months when Jewell had found that she had no one else to speak to, but she'd never expected McKenzie to actually come through.

"I am torn, Jewell, but this I can do with a clear conscious," McKenzie said quietly.

"Why are you torn?" Jewell asked.

"Please don't ask questions right now. Just go to the appointment and know that I'm wishing you the best of luck." McKenzie rattled off the name and address and time and then hung up.

Jewell stood there for a few moments and then felt herself smiling. She'd known when she woke that today would be a good day, and it was starting out the best way possible.

"Today *is* going to be a good day," she told herself out loud. All she had to do was make sure she exuded confidence. It would *all* be good. She left the apartment with a spring in her step. The attorney would tell her exactly what she wanted to hear. She was sure of it.

An hour later, Jewell wasn't feeling nearly as positive as she sat back in the stiff leather chair and listened to the man speak.

"The court asked for a visible change in your circumstances, Ms. Weston, a sign of stability. You don't have a positive employment history, and though you say you have money coming in, a one-time settlement won't show Judge Malone that you are ready and able to be responsible for this child. Since you lost the last battle with the courts, you're in an even more vulnerable position."

"How could the courts possibly think it would be better for my brother to be raised by strangers who don't care about him at all?" she gasped.

"It's not a matter of who will love your brother more. It's very black and white, and they don't want to see this boy bounced around for years until he ends up as yet another child in the juvenile-justice system."

Jewell did not like this man, not one little bit. McKenzie had said he was good, but all Jewell could see was that he was cold and he definitely wasn't saying what she wanted to hear. "I disagree with you, Mr. Sharp. I think my brother is much better off with a sister who loves him and will do whatever it takes to ensure his safety."

"I have been doing my job for a long time, Ms. Weston, and I won't take on a case that I'm sure to lose. I'm telling you now that this is a losing case." The way he said those words wasn't exactly cruel, but still they cut her to the bone.

Her stomach sank as she looked into his almost

sympathetic eyes. That was all she needed — pity. She'd have felt better if he'd sported a sneer, because the expression he wore told her she didn't have a chance in hell of winning this case on her own.

Dammit! That out-and-out bastard Blake Knight. He knew all of this. That's why he'd shown so much confidence when he told her she would do whatever he wanted.

Power.

It was that word again. It was something that Blake Knight had, and something she would never achieve. How she hated this constant sense of helplessness, of inevitable defeat.

"You are sure that there's nothing else I can do, Mr. Sharp?"

She didn't want to hear the attorney's next words, but she braced herself for them anyway.

"I'm sorry, Ms. Weston, but at this point, you don't have a winning case. If your life doesn't undergo drastic change, there's no reason for you to even try to reopen this case. Sadly, that means that your brother could very easily be swallowed up by the system."

Once again, she heard that depressing pity.

"What do you mean by *drastic*?" There was nothing she wouldn't do at this point.

"This is strictly off the record, but the courts want to see stability. They want to see two-parent households, and they want to know that household will remain intact and welcoming to the child. No more disruptions. You need a home, you need security, and you need a lot more than you are showing right now."

Jewell fully understood what he was telling her. She'd be on solid ground if she could tell the court that she had a husband, that she was a happily married woman who would provide a stable home for her brother. They didn't see an unemployed twenty-four-year-old who'd recently lived in a homeless shelter as someone suitable to raise a child. They didn't care if she had graduated from a top notch school, and left to take care of her ailing mother. All they cared about was where she was right at this moment.

She nearly laughed aloud at her own thoughts. Sure, it was a bitter laugh. She thought she'd already reached the point of hysteria, but as she saw the last of her hope slip away, she realized that she'd only scratched the surface of misery.

Jewell couldn't possibly imagine a world without her brother in it. But wasn't his happiness far more important than her own? Of course it was. And if he managed to find a family that would love him for the rest of his life, wouldn't he be happy? Maybe. But wouldn't he be happier with her?

Not if she couldn't provide him with a stable environment.

"I can't give him the home he needs, can I?" she asked Mr. Sharp. Even though this man didn't know her, sometimes it took a stranger to tell you the truth in a way that you could actually hear it.

"That's not what I'm saying, Ms. Weston. I don't know you. From the look in your eyes, I can see that you love your brother very much, but love, unfortunately, isn't always the answer, and love certainly doesn't put food on the table, or offer a roof over anyone's head."

"Ah, but love can turn mountains into molehills," she replied with more than a trace of sarcasm.

"In theory," he said with the slightest of smiles.

"What would your advice be for me to do next?"

The attorney paused for so long, she figured he was giving up on even talking to her. She was sure he wanted nothing more than for her to leave his office. At least this man hadn't led her on and taken her money.

He finally leaned forward and looked her in the eyes.

"If you can't lose him, do whatever it takes."

And those were the words with which she carried with her as left his office. No, he wouldn't represent her, and she had no doubt that, no matter how many attorneys she visited, her situation wouldn't improve.

So she was now left with a simple choice: to give up or to fight. Which was she going to do?

She made her way back to her new apartment. But it wasn't hers, was it? Nothing was. No matter what she seemed to achieve, she kept getting kicked back down.

Stop this right now! Jewell told herself. *You're not the kind of person to think this way.*

She wouldn't drown in her own defeat. There were some calls she needed to make. And when she was done, she knew she would feel a whole heck of a lot better.

Full of purpose, she stepped into her sitting room and then drew back a step. Sipping a cup of tea while sitting elegantly on Jewell's couch — well, Blake's couch, to be more accurate — was Ms. Beaumont.

"Hello, Jewell. How did the visit go?"

The woman's face didn't tell Jewell a single thing; it was closed and almost blank. Jewell wished she could be as sophisticated as this woman. Maybe it wasn't sophistication, though; maybe Ms. Beaumont was just a woman who had seen it all and was beyond feeling interest or excitement.

"I appreciate you setting it up," Jewell said, sitting across from her.

"You seem upset. It must not have gone well." She said it like she had known all along it wouldn't have gone well. Then why had she put Jewell through that? Because she knew Jewell would fight to the end, that was why.

"I'm just fine," she told Ms. Beaumont. Why not? There was nothing else the woman could do to make her feel better.

"I don't believe that, Jewell, but I won't pry. I understand. Besides, I value my privacy too much to invade someone else's."

"I appreciate it," Jewell replied. Then she couldn't take the suspense any longer. "Why are you here?" To any other person the words might have sounded rude, but Ms. Beaumont, Jewell knew, preferred it when people got right to the point.

"I have the first half of your payment," Ms. Beaumont said, and held out a check.

Jewell's heart raced, but she tried not to seem too eager to snatch the check up. "Why only half?" is what she asked instead.

"You will get the other half in thirty days."

"And what if he's not willing to let me go in thirty days?"

There was a very long pause, and Jewell could see that McKenzie knew more than she wanted to tell, but she also knew the woman would speak if she was given time.

"He only paid for thirty days, Jewell," McKenzie finally said.

"That wasn't my question," Jewell pointed out.

McKenzie sighed before looking Jewell in the eye.

"Ultimately, the choice is yours at the end of your time," she began before giving Jewell a sad but sympathetic smile. "But, as you know, men like Blake Knight hold a lot of power, and they tend to get what they want."

"I'm only too aware of that," Jewell said. "He's reminded me himself of the fact more than once. Just tell me what he's said to you."

"I can't," McKenzie said as she stood up.

"Please," Jewell begged as the woman moved toward the front door.

She turned to Jewell with sad eyes. "This world doesn't always give us the ending we deserve. Blake…" She stopped as she looked over Jewell's shoulder. "You may never be free." And then she was gone.

CHAPTER NINE

WHAT THE HECK was she doing? Jewell stared at the front door of Blake's penthouse. She'd stayed there for a week only, and that was months ago, yet the doorman had remembered her, and he'd allowed her up without hesitation.

That meant that Blake was either expecting her or he'd never told them she was no longer allowed in. She didn't know which would be better for her right now. But at the moment she couldn't think, she was so filled with worry and rage. Would she come off as stark mad? Probably. And maybe being hauled off to jail or a mental hospital was exactly what she needed. Then she could say she'd done everything she could for Justin, but it was now out of her hands.

No. She wouldn't do that. She wasn't one to give up, not without one hell of a fight. Still, she didn't know what this visit was going to accomplish. All she knew was that she was furious right now, and the person she wanted to take her anger out on was Blake.

When she heard the knock on his door, she jumped, and then was surprised to see her fist raised. *She* had been the one to knock. It almost felt as if she were a separate person, or a disembodied brain, watching this bizarre scene unfold.

What was wrong with her? Maybe a person really could snap. One too many kicks backward on the path of life and you just couldn't take it anymore.

When the door opened and she saw Blake right in front of her, she froze. If she'd worked out a script for what she'd do or say, she couldn't remember it now. He stood there in all his glory, wearing a low-slung pair of gray sweats but no shirt, and with his strong fingers gripping the towel hanging around his neck. He waited for her to say the first words.

She nearly stumbled backward and wasn't sure how she'd mustered the strength to keep from falling on her ass. She hated how breathtaking this man was, hated how he made her heart skip a beat even when she considered him the enemy, even when she knew he was the one in control of her life — at least for the next thirty days.

Without saying a word, he took a step back and beckoned, an invitation for her to come inside. All she could think of was the line "'Will you walk into my parlor?' said the Spider to the Fly." Not good.

Still, amid the oppressive silence, she found her feet moving, found herself being drawn forward into his web. She knew she might regret this later, but right now she was running on pure emotion, and even knowing that he was somehow controlling this game, she half considered herself the one in control, because she was here of her own free will — though her actions were fueled by rage and hopelessness.

He finally spoke. "I thought it would take longer for you to come to your senses and see that you need me," he told her with a smirk.

"You may have all the power, Blake, but I am my own woman and I will leave you when my jail sentence is over," she snapped.

"You think you will," he replied smugly, but the fire burning in his eyes said he was anything but calm.

"You can't keep me, Blake."

"I can keep whatever I choose to keep, Jewell, including you," he informed her, and edged closer.

All the agony of the past six months came to a head, and because he was the one standing before her, he would be the one to feel her wrath.

She never got the chance to unload on him.

With a growl of satisfaction, he grabbed her hair and pulled her forward, no gentleness in his touch as he showed her exactly who was in control. She knew that she should stop this, and that she was giving him exactly what he wanted by being in his apartment, but she couldn't pull away from him mentally any more than she could physically.

His lips took hers as he ground his hips against her, and she felt how hard he already was. Oh yes, Blake liked it rough, and he liked it kinky. *Plain vanilla* wasn't in his sexual vocabulary. And though she hated herself for it, she liked it the way he did.

Somehow she'd known this was exactly where the two of them were headed — even in all her fury she had known it. From the moment he'd made his magical reappearance in her world, the two of them had no other option but to end up right here.

He released her lips and she gasped for air, but nothing seemed to be tamping down this hunger, this passion, this raw craving that was rushing through her blood. This wasn't about sex; it was about need, the need to feel anything other than hopelessness.

Blake ran his hand down her back and pressed her against his bare chest, making her cry out as the thin material of her bra almost scratched her hardened nipples. She couldn't breathe, couldn't focus, couldn't figure out what she needed most.

"Quit thinking, Jewell. Do nothing but feel," he ordered her before tugging on her hair again and fusing their lips together once more.

And she did exactly as he commanded, letting her mind go blank as her body focused on the flood of sensations flowing through it. This man, only this man, knew how to make her forget the world, how to take her to the highest reaches of pleasure. It didn't matter if she hated herself for it. Whatever she did right now, she'd despise herself afterward. So why not take what pleasure she could in his arms? Why not push the pain away for a moment in time?

She whimpered in submission as he smoothed his hands down her back and cupped the sweet curves of her rear so he could pull her into his hardness. He grasped her bottom lip with his teeth and bit down just enough to send a flash of pain through her before his tongue soothed the spot and rocked her with new currents of desire.

Time stopped having meaning as his hands and lips created a perfect storm of desire all through her body, leaving her wet, needy and hungry for more.

When his lips released hers and he stepped back, she

moaned despairingly, but he didn't leave her for long. He threw the towel off his neck, then pushed her back against the wall, ripped her shirt and bra from her body, and pinned her hands above her head.

Jewell hardly noticed when Blake stripped off her pants and her panties, and she was standing with him, his naked chest pressed into hers, her nipples rubbing against his smooth, solid skin, his hands squeezing the flesh of her behind, his mouth owning hers.

When she thought she couldn't possibly take any more without crumpling at his feet, his lips skimmed down her neck, then over her heaving breasts, and he took each nipple into his mouth just long enough to make them bead out in pleasure. And then he was dropping to his knees and nuzzling her stomach with his mouth.

"Blake…," she cried out, digging her fingers into his hair. She didn't know what she was asking of him, but he certainly did.

Moving lower, he worshipped the sensitive skin right above her heated core, caressing her skin with his tongue, and his fingers opened her up to his demanding mouth.

Her internal temperature soared as he sucked her swollen bud and his tongue swiped against it, once… twice…a third time, and more, until she lost count. She suddenly felt the explosion rip through her, her core tightening around the fingers he was using to stroke her G-spot, and her legs threatening to buckle as wave after wave of release overtook her.

Before the last of her tremors died away, he surged to his feet and caught her hips in his strong hands, lifting her against the wall and swinging her legs around him. His manhood was ready for action, and he pulled her down his length, coating himself with her pleasure, before lifting her back up and then pushing her down hard around him. Her eyes widened and a gasp of pleasure escaped, and she found herself meeting his desire-filled gaze.

"You are so tight, so perfect, my Jewell," he groaned as he kept withdrawing and then plunging back inside her.

He lost every shred of control. He dug his fingers tightly into her hips as he thrust in and out of her, the friction and franticness of their lovemaking sending her rapidly toward an even more explosive finish than the last.

Jewell grasped his shoulders, leaned her head against his neck, and bit the salty skin of his shoulder while he continued pumping in and out with such force that she wasn't sure how the wall behind her remained standing.

"Oh, please, Blake, please…" She had to beg him for release — the intensity of their union was just too much to bear for even a minute longer.

With a few more thrusts, he gave her exactly what she needed, and this time she saw fireworks behind her tightly closed eyes as her body contracted and pulsed around him and she screamed her ecstasy into the flesh of his now bruised shoulder.

It took a moment before she realized he too was shaking as he cried out in his own intense release and sent his ejaculation shuddering through her, her womb growing even hotter as his seed coated her insides.

When it was all over, she slumped against him, her legs frozen to his back — the only thing that kept her from falling. Her body felt like a mass of jelly, and she was afraid that if he released her, she'd slide down the wall into a boneless heap, never able to get up again.

"I need more," he groaned against the top of her head.

How? There was nothing else she could possibly give, nothing else he could give either. Their joining had been soul- and body-shattering, and if they attempted to continue as they'd begun, neither of them might make it out in one piece.

She was beginning to drift out of consciousness when some sort of movement jarred her awake. Was it them, or had an earthquake hit in Seattle? She lacked the strength to open her eyes to find out. But then his arms released her and she felt herself falling backward.

Her eyes opened with a start when she landed against the coolness of his sheets, his scent instantly flooding her and unbelievably setting off another rumble of need low in her belly.

He'd only pushed his sweatpants out of the way when he made love to her before; she watched as he shed them, and now he was on top of her, his eyes staring intently into hers as he spread her legs with his knees, and poised his arousal — still hard! — above her core.

"What? We can't…," she cried as he slipped the tip of his manhood inside her swollen folds.

"Not only can we, Jewell, but we will." He thrust inside and wrenched a moan of pleasure from deep within her.

He lay full against her now, gripping the back of her thigh with one hand and pulling her leg up, opening her to him so he could slide all the way in, up to the hilt.

Soon he was thrusting his tongue in and out of her mouth in perfect rhythm with his body, making her stomach quiver as the pleasure rose almost unbearably higher.

As he moved his hips skillfully, his hardness filling her in ways only he could fill her — and only he had —

she convulsed around him countless times, shattering in immeasurable pleasure. She didn't want this night to end, and didn't want the pleasure to ever stop.

Now slowing, and now speeding back up, Blake made love to her in a way he never had before in their times together. Yes, there was desperation, and yes, there was urgency, but there were also moments of tenderness, and of passion beyond anything she could imagine.

His tongue traced her swollen lips, his words washed over her skin, his body fit perfectly against hers, and she begged him to never stop. When he finally pulled from her, he trailed his lips down her neck, took her peaked nipples into his mouth and, instead of soothing them, made them ache even more. Then he moved downward and tasted their passion on his tongue before climbing back up to the top of the bed and allowing her to taste it too.

And now he was over her again, slipping back inside her swollen core and commanding her to look at him. "Open your eyes, Jewell. I want to see the explosion in them. Do not close them under any circumstance!"

She tried to disobey, but he bit her lip lightly, causing her to gasp, and she was too weak to fight him. Her eyes were almost slits, but they stayed open as he moved faster and faster, building up the pressure within her once again.

And then she came apart. As the climax tore savagely through her, taking every last bit of energy she had left, she gazed into his nearly black eyes and watched their depths sparkle with satisfaction. She and Blake went up in a blaze of ecstasy and their voices rang out together in perfect harmony.

And Jewell could take no more. She gave in gladly to

the compelling darkness.

CHAPTER TEN

BLAKE WAS STILL lying on top of Jewell, and he knew the second she lost consciousness. She obviously needed to rest, to be left alone, as the passion had drained her, but the thought of leaving her caused him actual physical pain — the need churning up his insides seemed insatiable. He'd spent three months thinking of no other woman but her, and during that time he had felt...*bereft.* That was the only word that captured it. He suspected he'd be feeling the effects of that loss for a long time to come. Even knowing what he knew, he felt that way, and it infuriated him.

Why? How? He had no idea. No woman had ever lodged herself so deeply and firmly inside him. Not even close. He'd never allowed such a thing to happen. What made Jewell different? Why did it seem that he'd never get enough of her?

He tried to reason it away, tried to tell himself it was nothing but raw hunger, but wouldn't hunger eventually fade away with repeated satiation? So maybe what the two of them had would fade, but for now, it was all-consuming and he couldn't say that he didn't love every minute of it.

This woman had barreled into his life and in a minuscule amount of time had shaken him to the core. Blake hadn't thought that was possible. He'd thought he was so hardened by the traumas of his past that no woman would be able to make him feel. And he had to remember she was a liar. He had to have answers. But none of that seemed to matter to him when she was in his arms. And that made him feel like an even bigger fool. But he couldn't seem to stop himself when it came to her. He could tell himself it was to get answers. But there was more to it than just that.

Rolling gently off Jewell, he lay at her side and watched his hand trail down her body. He'd taken her for what seemed like hours, had released twice inside of her heat, but only now was he feeling even a modicum of relief from that damnable sexual tension that had dogged him since he'd first met her. And as he continued to touch her soft skin with light fingers, he felt himself begin stirring again.

As he watched Jewell's eyelashes flutter, he knew for certain he couldn't let her go, not any time in the near future, at least. And that had nothing to do with needing answers, dammit! Of course he held the power to keep her beside him. He knew her primary weakness, and she needed him to cater to it. Did he feel at all guilty that he was using her brother to get her loyalty? No. Because he didn't trust her when it came to Justin. He justified his actions because he wanted her and he was going to have her any way that he possibly could. And damn the consequences, damn the cost to himself or to anyone else.

His heart had stopped its frantic thudding, and his

breathing had slowed, but he knew both would go back into overdrive the moment he sank back inside of her glorious heat. When would he ever have enough? Never was impossible, but he knew too well what "they" said about saying *never*.

Her eyes floated open, and she looked dazed and sated. For one moment her guard was down. Maybe that was the key. He would simply keep her in his bed, where he could look into her depths when she was too defenseless to hold him at bay. But the problem with that, was that when she was like this, he was also vulnerable. He couldn't afford that.

Blake wasn't a weak man — he didn't back down from a challenge. And Jewell Weston was most definitely a challenge. He wanted her obedience, and he wanted her pleasure. They belonged to him. But he also wanted them to come from her of her own free will, not because they were forced upon her. And the last thing he could do, if he were to be honest with himself, was make her hate him. But since when? Since seeing her again?

Though he could be ready to take her in moments, he also felt a perverse need to talk to her, to connect in a way that he hadn't ever before connected with another human. Yes, he loved his brothers, but there was a limit to how far he let even them in. Why didn't he find he was setting such a limit with Jewell? He'd have to fight against this dangerous impulse.

He leaned over her and spoke. "You know that this is just the beginning, Jewell. I missed you. My body missed you, and I feel as if I can't get enough of you. I'm not sure right now whether I ever will."

He took the utmost delight in the widening of her eyes,

in her shocked intake of breath. Then he looked down at her hardening nipples and felt pride in knowing he could turn her on with nothing but words.

He caressed her nipples with his palm, felt them harden even more under his touch. "You are mine. You have to know that. I'm the only one who's ever brought you this pleasure, and I'm the only one who can." He lowered his head, and when his mouth took the place of his hand, her exquisite flavor made his taste buds explode. She gasped as he moved his hand down her stomach and ran his fingers along the outside of her core.

"No. I…uh…I have to leave…," she gasped, shutting her legs weakly and trapping his hand.

He knew how easily he could pry her legs back open, and how quickly he could have her begging him to take her, but that's not what he wanted. He wanted her to initiate this too, wanted her to need him as much as he needed her. He wanted her to give herself freely, without any coercion on his part. He didn't want to remind her that he'd bought her and he didn't have to let her go.

What in the world was wrong with him?

"I don't want you to leave," he said, removing his hand and resting it on her shaking stomach.

"I…I can't think, Blake. Please stop touching me."

The hint of desperation in her voice made him pause. Though it pained him to pull back, he did, but only after thrusting his tongue out to get one final taste of her nipple before he released her.

"You don't need to think, Jewell. When you're in my bed, all you need to do is feel." Okay, he could admit that sounded corny! To save face, he was left with no choice but to accompany his words with a cocky smile, one that instantly irritated her.

For some reason, he couldn't seem to stop pushing her buttons, even when he actually wanted to stop. Maybe it was because the fire in her eyes turned him on, and maybe it was his armor locking into place, but whatever the reason, he could see that she was pulling back from him. He refused to show her that it mattered to him.

"I came here for a reason," she said, reaching for a blanket and covering herself, much to his disappointment.

"And that reason was accomplished," he told her with another confident smile.

"I didn't come here to screw you, Blake," she told him, scorn dripping from her tongue.

He leaned in even closer, making her eyes fly wide open. "Oh, Jewell, don't lie to me or to yourself — I won't allow it. You can't honestly tell me that you didn't come here knowing you'd end up in my bed."

When her breath caught in her throat and she was at a loss for any comebacks, only then did he sit up and fold his hands behind his head as if he had nothing more important to do than hang out in his bed with a raging erection while the two of them chatted.

Blake had to grin when he noticed her eyes straying to his arousal before darting back up to his face. "You can climb on and take me for a ride if you want to," he remarked, and those words earned him a glare.

"How can a person think about nothing but sex?" she said with a frustrated sigh.

"I find it very easy when I have such a captivating partner, Jewell."

"We have to talk," she told him.

"That is the last thing I'm in the mood for right now,"

he replied.

"You can only keep me in a sex coma for so long, Blake."

Throwing up his hands in defeat, he backed off, which surprised him. This woman made him do things he wasn't willing to do, and what bothered him most about that was that it didn't actually bother him.

"So, what do we need to discuss?" Blake finally asked her.

"My brother. What else?" she said as she gripped the blankets tightly against her luscious breasts. He'd so hoped that she would let the damned covers slip.

"I told you I'll help you to see him."

"But how? I want to know how."

"I know people," he said. He couldn't tell her his plans yet, couldn't make things happen too quickly, or he would never have answers. And then she would be gone from his life. That he couldn't allow.

His arousal died down as the depressing topic drove away any thoughts of sex. Blake stood up and yanked on his sweats, frustrated that his evening wasn't going the way he had hoped.

"You got your sex. Now give me my brother," she demanded, her words stopping him where he stood at the foot of the bed and causing his eyes to narrow briefly.

He carefully turned his face into a blank so she wouldn't see what her words were doing to him. He did want sex, that was true, and for her to trade her body for her brother is what he'd asked of her. So why did he feel as if he'd been punched in the gut?

Ridiculous. That's what it was. He wouldn't tolerate weakness in himself. If she wanted to play dirty, then dirty is what she would get.

"Do you really think I'm that easy, Jewell?" he asked in a deadly cold voice. She flinched, and he refused to let it make him feel a single thing.

"Yes. I think that you're an emotionless drone and you'll do anything it takes to get what you want. You wanted sex. You got it. I want my brother. I think I've earned the right to get what you offered." Her chin tilted up in the stubborn way it did when she was terrified but trying to hide it. How was it that he knew so much about her when he'd spent so little time with her?

He couldn't answer that question. Maybe it was because he hadn't seemed to be able to think of anything or anyone else but her since the moment he'd walked into that sleeping area at the escort agency and seen her sitting up in that small bed. That was until he'd also found out about Justin. Then, he'd only been able to think about both of them.

"Do you really think you've done enough for me to let you go? I have you for an entire month, Jewell — at least."

Again she flinched, and again he refused to let up on her. If she saw how weak he really was when it came to her, she would be the one with all the power. That was simply unacceptable.

"I do," she said, the words barely above a whisper.

"You aren't a stupid woman, Jewell, not at all. So why do you insist on acting like one?"

"I'm not acting stupid. I'm trying to get you to honor your word," she replied.

"If you think I'm letting you go this easily, you aren't displaying a shred of intelligence. Don't forget that I paid a quarter of a million dollars for the privilege of doing anything I want with you. Your *services* didn't come cheap, sweetheart. Mine won't either."

He turned away as he took a deep breath. Unbelievably, this conversation was taking a lot out of him. It shouldn't have been. He was letting her upset him and that wasn't even a little okay.

"So you threaten me, bribe me, then get what you want and won't hold up to your word?"

That made his hands clench into fists. When he felt the urge to slam them into the wall, he knew this conversation had best end soon. It wasn't going at all the way it ought to. Finally, he turned back around and the look on his face must not have been as composed as he had thought it was, because she seemed to shrivel down into the bed.

"Believe me, Jewell, if I threaten or blackmail you in any way, there will be no doubt that I'm doing so. I don't need to hide my words in secret meanings. I don't need to beat around the bush. I will express myself very loudly and clearly, and I will get exactly what I want," he said harshly.

But that wasn't exactly true. They were both lying to each other. He didn't say that.

"But I did what you wanted," she practically cried.

"You haven't even tapped the surface of what I want!"

She glared at him while she struggled to find words with which to answer him, and he was eager to hear what she would say next. With Jewell, he really had no idea. She was obviously feeling forced into a corner, but that was good right now. Sometimes that was what it took to make people go outside their comfort zone. She wanted him. She just felt that she had to be pushed to accept that. He could live with being the one to push her.

Her expression hardened. "How long will you want me in your bed, Blake?" She was waiting for a number.

The question made him smile. No, not a real smile, but a smile of a shark about to snatch its prey.

"Do you really want to hear my answer, Jewell?" he asked, his lips turning up even more.

"What? A month? A year?"

"Ah, Jewell, you underestimate yourself. Do you really want to see your brother? Will you *really* do whatever it takes?" He refused to even think about the small sting of regret his atrophied conscience might try to make him feel over his next words. Look, this was just another business deal. It didn't make him a monster.

"Yes, I'm willing to do whatever it takes, Blake. You obviously know that." Her voice dripped with loathing.

"Good." He said the word and then turned his back on her as if the conversation were done.

She jumped from the bed, jerking on the blanket and wrapping it awkwardly around her delectable body.

"Don't walk away from me, Blake. Tell me what you want," she demanded.

He faced her again and pulled her into his arms, kissing her breathless before he spoke. "If you want your brother, then you will forget about Relinquish Control and the auction and you will remain mine."

"I don't understand."

"I'm not letting you go, Jewell — maybe ever. Quit planning your escape, quit trying to leave me, and just agree to belong to me." He didn't even know where these words were coming from. This hadn't been what he had planned on saying. She just triggered his emotions to the extreme.

"I don't belong to anyone. And what makes you think that I would keep my word? I could tell you anything you want to hear right now, and then walk out anyway," she pointed out.

That stopped him for a moment. She was correct. What could he do that would ensure she wouldn't leave until he had everything he wanted? He paused as he looked down at her and then he got an idea. No. That was ridiculous. It was something he'd vowed never to do, not even after… never mind that. So he was just as shocked as Jewell when the next words emerged from his mouth.

"Marry me and I'll give you your brother."

When her mouth dropped open, she was incapable of speech, so Blake decided to kiss her again. In his book, after all, she'd just consented and it was time to seal the deal.

CHAPTER ELEVEN

WHOOSH! HER LUNGS were robbed of oxygen. She really had to have heard Blake wrong — he couldn't have just told her the price she'd have to pay to get her brother back was marriage to him.

Why in the world would he want to marry her?

When he finally released her from his grasp, she stumbled backward, still clutching the blanket to her as if her life depended on it. Maybe it did. Everyone talked about security blankets. This blanket represented her sanity, and if she lost her hold on this fine bit of fabric, she would also lose her hold on her mind. Heck, that made as much sense as Blake's demand that she marry him.

And yet these strange thoughts gave her new determination, and she changed her focus. She wouldn't reply to his off-the-wall proposal. If she didn't reply, then it was a nonissue, right? Of course it was. So instead of looking at the wretched man, she moved away from him and went off to get her clothes, which were strewn around back in his front hall. Somehow managing to keep a grip on her blanket, she reached out with her other hand and gathered up her clothing, some of it rather the worse for wear…and tear.

Maintaining a resolute silence, she walked to his bathroom and firmly shut the door. The next thing she knew, she was in the shower. How had that happened? One second she was thinking she needed to get clean, she had to get clean, and then the next, hot water was cascading over her.

When she realized she was still clutching her so-called security blanket, she let it fall to the shower floor and kicked it into the corner, where its luxurious silk now lay ruined. She peeked through the glass doors and was grateful to see she'd at least dropped her clothes on the bathroom floor.

If she hadn't, she'd be wringing them out and putting them on as they were, and then wandering outside cold, wet and confused. Just to cap everything off, of course, the police would surely pick her up and haul her down to the station, and they'd probably treat her like the prostitute that she was. With those happy reflections, she washed her hair and kept scrubbing her body, and when the bathroom was thick with steam, she shut off the water, climbed out of the massive shower, and took her sweet time in toweling off.

When her clothes were back firmly in place, offering her a measure of protection from Blake — yeah, right, just like they had earlier — she decided she couldn't hide out in his bathroom any longer. She needed to get out of his apartment so she could *try* to figure out what in the world she was going to do next.

Why had his words shocked her so much? She didn't know. It wasn't as if she planned on marrying someday — especially now, given her recent job history — so why should a piece of paper upset her? Maybe because at one time in her life, marriage had actually meant something special. It had been a cherished dream of hers to fall in love, have a dream wedding with a meaningful church ceremony, and then have a few children and two cats in the yard. But that dream had seemed to die around the time she had buried her mother.

Maybe, in spite of it all, there was still a small piece of her that held hope of a "brighter tomorrow." But with Blake eclipsing the sun from her life, that wasn't likely. Maybe she just needed to accept that some people didn't get the fairy tale they thought they deserved.

Yet Jewell knew deep down inside, and had known it even when in her darkest moments of despair, that life would change, that someday things would eventually even out and she'd have days of true happiness. Sometimes, though, that seemed a deluded fantasy.

What she really didn't understand at all was what he'd get out of marrying her. He could have anyone; he could be with the wealthiest of the wealthy, with landed aristocrats, and even with royalty. What in the world would ever make him even think of tying himself down with her? She was a nobody who could do nothing for him.

When she finally slipped on her shoes, she got ready to flee, but when she reached the front door, she found him standing there, his face a mask.

There was no way of escaping unless she suddenly developed some prize football prowess and could knock him on his ass and rush over his stunned body. That thought nearly made her smile — almost, but not quite.

"I need to go," she said, standing far enough away that he couldn't snake out his arms and grab her.

"You haven't responded to my request yet, Jewell. You're the one who wanted to talk, and when I did talk, you rushed off into another room for an hour and then you headed straight for the front door. To me, that's not talking." He had propped himself up against the door, and the doorknob was hidden behind him.

Taking a calming breath, Jewell looked at his nose, knowing better than to meet his eyes. "Yes, I wanted to talk. I was wrong. I...this...I can't think," she stammered, frustrated that she couldn't find the words she was searching for. "You already have me in your bed. I don't understand why you want more than that. It doesn't make sense, and my head is too muddled right now to try to make anything make sense, so I need to just be alone. *Please*."

He didn't move.

So much for attempting to reason with him, she thought bitterly. "Look, Blake, I'll do anything to get my brother back, but that doesn't mean you have to marry me to continue getting me in your bed. You paid for me, remember? Of course you do. You reminded me of it earlier in your inimitable way. Hell, I know that I wouldn't quickly forget paying a quarter of a million dollars for someone or something. Ms. Beaumont was quite specific: I have to make you happy. But now...I just...I need to go *right now*."

He still didn't move, which made her even more nervous.

"Why don't you want to marry me, Jewell?"

She stopped squirming and finally looked in his eyes, but as usual, his expression showed her nothing.

"Because even though I'll probably never get married, the act of marriage still means something to me. It's not a charade, and though a lot of people seem to see it as simply a virtually meaningless piece of paper legally binding two people until they tire of each other, I was taught that it's more than that…"

"Our marriage will be real," he told her calmly.

"There won't be a marriage, Blake. I don't know when or how you got this idea, but it's not going to happen," she said, her voice rising.

"I met with the judge, Jewell, and he told me that because you didn't meet the conditions the court set at the first hearing, you would have zero chance of getting your brother back unless you were married to a solid member of the community."

What he said knocked her feet right out from under him. This was too close to what the attorney had said to her.

"I…I…How can they put that sort of condition on getting custody? It's wrong," she said, her head spinning.

"It is what it is, Jewell." He was speaking so casually — as if he had conversations like this every day.

"What's in this for you?"

He looked at her intently and for several moments she didn't know whether he was going to answer her or not. She remained silent, too, since she didn't know what she could possibly say at this point.

Then when he finally opened his mouth, she wished he hadn't.

"I'm working on a big deal with a company in a

conservative country," he said. "The owner doesn't trust bachelors, thinking they are either gay or out to prey on other men's wives. So, you see, this works for both of us quite nicely."

"Why me, though? Why on earth would you marry someone like me? I'm sure you could find a hundred other women — socially acceptable women — who wouldn't hesitate to take your name, and you'd lock in this deal with no problem."

"But I want you. And you need me. It's that simple," he said. "This way we both get something important to us, and you won't have the constant urge to run and hide."

"I could still run, even if we were married," she pointed out.

"Not if we both have custody of Justin."

"You actually think I would give up my rights to him as soon as I get them back?" she gasped.

"You won't get them back without me, Jewell."

This was what she'd been afraid of. If what he was saying about the judge was true, she had no hope without Blake. So, why even fight this anymore?

"What sort of man are you?"

"I'm the sort of man who knows what he wants and goes for it."

"Well, you can't own another person, Blake."

"You're very wrong there, Jewell. I can own you. I do own you," he told her coldly, and the shiver that ran through her veins had nothing to do with the temperature of the room.

Her eyes narrowed and flashed danger. "I do so hate you," she grated out.

"I don't need love from you, Jewell. I need your

compliance, your truth, and I need your body," he said with an unreadable smirk. "And I'll even give you a day or two to think about whether you're willing to give those things to me."

Gee, wasn't he magnanimous!

"Do you really know what you're trying to get yourself into? Do you know how much work caring for a child is, especially one who has been through the traumas that Justin has? You can't do whatever you want whenever you want to if you have one living in your home. They are messy, they are demanding, and they are exhausting. Why don't you give me back my brother, and then go and find some easy woman, one who is willing to bend all the rules for you? Why are you hell-bent on making a bad situation even worse?"

"I've already said this to you numerous times, Jewell. I want you, and I won't change my mind."

The steel in his voice told her that he was speaking the truth, and the anxiety in her stomach told her the same thing. He wasn't going to back down from this — not unless it was his idea.

"You aren't really giving me a choice and you know it."

"I've told you what I want and expect, Jewell. Anyway, you're not for sale, because you've already been sold — to me. But because I'm such a stand-up guy, I'll let you think about it." With those words, he took a step toward her. She stepped back in fear, but then he turned away, leaving the way wide open for her to make a quick exit.

Was this a trap? She wouldn't put it past him. She was afraid that if she went to the door, he'd strike like a python and swallow her whole.

Moving quickly, she yanked open the door and had

taken a step toward freedom when she felt his fingers grip her arm. Yep. She'd been right to think he wouldn't release her that quickly. She also knew she had no real power left to resist him.

"Something to remind you of what we have together," he said before his lips descended and he was kissing her breath away again. When she swayed toward him, he released her. "We're good together, Jewell. We both know that in the end you'll bend to my will, but if you need to fight this to make yourself feel better, take the time to do it. There's no doubt in my mind that you're already mine."

With that, he stepped back once again, indicating with a gesture that she could go or she could stay.

She fled.

Jewell didn't know if she'd ever stop running, and she didn't even know who she was running from more — Blake or herself.

CHAPTER TWELVE

JEWELL SOMEHOW MADE it back to her apartment building. After stumbling inside and finally getting into her own front hall, she took extra time to fasten all the locks on the door.

Not that the strongest of locks would keep Blake out, especially since the man had the keys to the apartment, but the symbolism of doing it made her feel immeasurably better. She headed to her bedroom and fell onto the bed, where she knew she'd lie for hours without the possibility of sleep claiming her.

Hadn't she promised Justin that she'd get him back any way she could? Yes. So why in the world was she balking at marriage? It was selfish of her, and she knew it. Her brother was the only one who mattered. He was the reason she had gone to Relinquish Control in the first place. He was the reason she had met Blake.

No, she wasn't blaming her brother. Not at all. She was an adult and she'd made her choices. She'd had a great life while growing up. It was time for her brother to have that same privilege.

She tossed and turned the entire night, and when she did find a few minutes of peace in slumber, nightmares of her brother being dragged away from her woke her up. At the crack of dawn, when her chances of more sleep had hit nil, Jewell gave up on sleep.

She could continue to fight Blake, but he would always win. He had power, and she had absolutely none. It was why he hadn't been worried about what her answer would be. That the man had told her he'd give her time to think was almost amusing. It was like giving a starving animal a choice whether to eat or not. No matter how distrustful they were, they'd eventually take the food that was being handed to them.

Yes, she should call Blake and tell him he'd won. She should just get the damned thing over with. But she put it off. Maybe she was holding out hope that he'd change his mind, that he'd get tired of playing this game with her and he would release her from this hell.

But if that were to happen, where would she go? Sure, she had the money Ms. Beaumont had given her already, but it wasn't enough to save Justin and give them a new life. She had to face facts — she had nowhere, and no one else was about to help her but Blake.

Jewell climbed out of bed, wandered off to her kitchen and watched the coffee drip into the pot. The morning ritual gave her a measure of comfort, and how pathetic was that?

When the coffee was ready and poured, she added a nice splash of flavored cream, then found herself sitting in the living room gazing at one of the soulless, impersonal art pieces hanging on the stark white walls. So expensive, and yet so utterly lacking in real value…

She was filled with something almost like relief when the doorbell rang. Then she remembered that the only person who knew she lived there — besides Ms. Beaumont, of course — was Blake, and she wasn't ready to go another round with him. But why put off the inevitable? He was ringing the bell as a courtesy. He would get in whether she answered the bell or not.

When she opened the door, her face went from defeated to surprised as she looked up to see Tyler Knight, Blake's younger brother, standing there. Before she was able to say a word, he flashed her a big smile and pulled her into his arms.

"Ha. I've missed ya, Jewell." His affection for her was obvious.

She hadn't realized they were fast friends, and his enthusiasm at seeing her really threw her off balance. Tyler was certainly as good-looking as his brother, with wide shoulders, dark, slightly messy hair, and a dimple in his cheek that gave him a boyish charm neither of his brothers could even try to possess. He also was the first to smile and show his emotions, whereas Blake and the other Knight brother, Byron, made a point of playing everything close to the vest.

All three brothers were far more handsome than was good for them or the poor females who happened to stumble into their paths. And what made it even harder to resist them was the command, the raw strength that radiated from them in waves. There was something about a man who knew exactly who he was that made a woman want to give him anything and everything he could ever possibly desire.

"What are you doing here?" she finally asked when her stunned silence lasted a moment too long. *Oh, no*, she told herself and blushed. *How rude can you get?*

Tyler didn't twit her for her awkwardness, though. "I found out you were here," he said. "My brother slipped up. I think he was planning on keeping you all to himself, but I've always been pretty damn good at getting information that people have no intention of giving out. And since I haven't seen you in months, I decided to pop in for a little unannounced visit. That way you couldn't possibly turn me away. Hey! Is that fresh coffee I smell?" Without waiting for an invitation or an answer, he walked inside and made his way to her kitchen.

Jewell followed and found him rummaging through her cupboards for a mug. Then he grabbed her empty mug from her and poured them each fresh coffee. Smiling, she added cream to hers and led Tyler over to the kitchen table.

"Don't you have work or something much more important to do than sitting around and chatting with me, Tyler?"

"We can trade small talk all day long, Jewell, but why don't you just cut to the chase and tell me why you were gone for three months, why my brother was a bear during those months, and why now you have crater-sized dark circles under your eyes?" He softened the interrogation with a wink and a grin.

Jewell's own smile vanished while he spoke. She feared this man because she knew he had a way about him that would make the floodgates come flying open. And because he was Blake's brother, she shouldn't think for a minute that she could rely on him, no matter how nice he was to her.

"I think your brother can answer all of those questions," she told him with a brittle laugh.

Tyler reached across the table and took her hand. "I'm not asking Blake. I'm asking you."

She was so close to tears that she had to turn her head away. If only she had a single friend she could talk to. She couldn't even talk to McKenzie about this, because even though they had a strange friendship, she didn't fully trust her. But if she had someone then maybe she wouldn't feel this incessant urge to spill her guts to Blake's brother. But it was so difficult to hold everything in when he was looking at her with those openly friendly eyes.

"It's complicated," she finally said, and he let out a sigh.

"I'm not going to pretend that I can possibly understand everything, Jewell, but I have been able to tell from the first moment I met you that you're a good person. And though I love my brother very much, I know he can sometimes give people the wrong impression of who he is. There's a long story here, but it isn't my place to tell it."

"If he's so bitter, why aren't you?" she asked, wondering how two brothers could be so very different.

"I was too young to be affected as badly as Blake and Byron were by the disasters of our past. Then as I got older and saw the hell they were going through, I decided that I had a choice of being happy or angry. I much prefer happiness. Sometimes it really helps to get things off your chest, to talk to someone. The shrinks might call it cathartic."

The man was practically begging her to open up to him, and she was tempted, so tempted, to do just that. But what if it backfired on her and made her situation worse? Oh, wait. How much worse could it get?

Before she was able to stop herself, Jewell found herself opening her mouth and letting the entire story spill from her lips. To his credit, Tyler didn't interrupt a single time. His eyes narrowed, and he gripped his coffee cup tightly a few times, but he didn't release her hand, and he didn't ask any questions.

"…so last night, he demanded marriage, and really, I don't have any prospects of ever getting married to anyone else, so what difference should it make? But at the same time, I still believe in the institution, of two becoming one in the eyes of God and all that, and…I don't know. I'm just confused right now." Her long, sad story now finished, she was trying desperately not to give in to tears.

Jewell had been around Tyler only a couple of times now, but she couldn't have imagined seeing such fury on his normally happy face. With his eyes now slits and his mouth pressed firmly into a frown, the man was just as frightening as his two brothers. She wondered whether he realized it.

A shudder passed through her. Maybe she should have just kept quiet. Heck, there was no maybe about it. She shouldn't have spilled her guts to Blake's brother.

"I'm sorry," she said, her voice barely above a whisper.

"Oh, Jewell, I'm the one who's sorry. You've been shouldering far too much for far too long. I know that Blake must have honorable intentions toward you now, but he is certainly not going about it in the right way. You have done nothing wrong by talking to me. Let *me* handle my brother."

The way he said the last sentence sent a serious chill down her spine. "I don't want to come between your brother and you," she gasped, gripping his hand tightly with hers, panic in her eyes.

"My brothers and I may not always see eye to eye on things, but nothing will rip us apart, I assure you." Tyler's lips finally turned up just the slightest, but his eyes remained grim.

"Tyler, I'm so sorry. Really I am. Can't you just forget that I told you any of this?"

"It can't be undone, Jewell, and it shouldn't be. You need someone in your corner. I will speak with my brother — I guarantee you that." He stood up purposefully.

"Right now?" she squealed. She'd screwed up terribly, and she had to stop him before things got worse.

"The sooner, the better," he told her, and he started off toward her front door.

"Tyler, I really don't think this is a good idea." This would only infuriate Blake, make him even more exasperated with her than he already was.

"I guarantee there won't be any backlash, Jewell," Tyler said, and then he was gone, her front door closing behind him with a loud click.

Jewell walked into her sitting room and slumped down on the sofa, praying she hadn't just lost her only way to get Justin back. She had no idea what was going to happen next. What if Blake just gave up completely on her and she lost Justin forever because of it?

She'd have only herself to blame.

But there was nothing she could do now. Once one of the Knight men had his mind set on something, there was no turning back the clock. All she could do now was wait and see what Blake's next move would be. The waiting might well kill her…

CHAPTER THIRTEEN

TYLER SURE IS a strange one, Blake told himself for the umpteenth time as he neared the office building he shared with his brothers. Tyler had called an hour earlier, cursing him out like wildfire, calling him all sorts of names, and that wasn't at all like the guy. Blake was amazed not to feel more irritated about it.

Tyler was their peacemaker, the one who never lost his cool. From a few of the things his brother had growled at him, Blake had no doubt that Tyler had been to see Jewell and that she had told him everything. Instead of being pissed off about it, Blake was happy to see, or at least suspect, she hadn't lost all her fight. He wasn't sure how he felt about Tyler's being so protective of Jewell, but Blake also knew Tyler would never try to overstep his bounds with Jewell. The brothers never poached on each other's territory, though they weren't beyond pretending to do so.

As he neared the executive offices, he wondered what Tyler would say. The funny thing was that if Blake would listen to anyone other than Max, it would be one of his brothers, and especially Tyler, since Tyler was always the voice of reason when anger seemed to consume Blake to the depths of his soul — if he even had a soul. But Tyler sure as hell hadn't been the voice of reason an hour ago. He'd been too busy yelling.

Blake walked to his own office and decided to wait there for a while before buzzing his brother. It was such a rarity to find Tyler in a bad mood that Blake couldn't help but fuel the fire. Granted, that move might come back to bite him in the ass, but he couldn't help himself. A man had to do what a man had to do!

After about ten minutes his intercom sounded and he had no doubt it was Tyler. Tyler had most likely told the security staff to notify him the minute Blake entered the building.

"Yes, Tyler?" Blake said in a chipper tone.

Tyler replied gruffly. "We're supposed to be meeting, Blake."

Blake leaned back. "I'm sitting here waiting for you, bro."

The line disconnected and Blake could practically hear Tyler's chair hit the wall as his brother stood up and stomped from the office he had down at the end of the hall.

Blake schooled his expression and watched as his door was thrust open and Tyler came storming into the room.

"I've known you to do some pretty dumb-ass things in your lifetime, Blake, but this has got to be a new low for you."

No word of greeting.

"It's been a few days, brother," Blake told him with a smile. "It's good to see you, too."

"Don't try to play games with me, Blake. I'm not one of the idiots who bow and scrape to you, and fall at your feet." Tyler looked ready to throw a punch as he leaned across Blake's desk and glared at him.

Blake just laughed. His brother would get to the point eventually.

"Do you like being feared?" Tyler asked.

This question actually took Blake by surprise, and he lost just a trace of his grin. "Yes," he said, but was that still as true today as it had been a year ago — heck, even a few months ago? He honestly didn't know. Didn't inspiring fear equal power? That's what he'd always thought, anyway.

"And do you like scaring women and little children?"

"I'm not trying to scare Jewell." Blake was quickly growing weary of this line of conversation.

"Whether you're trying or not, you have her scared, alone, and desperate," Tyler said. Some of the fight drained from him now, and he moved back and sat, not looking away, just looking slightly sad that his brother would do this.

It shamed Blake more than he would ever admit. "I'm good to Jewell," he said in his own defense.

"If she's only with you out of fear, that's not being good to her, Blake. You have to earn someone's love and trust, not demand it of them."

"I don't need her love or her trust. I just need her." Blake wasn't willing to delve into his emotions with his brother. This wasn't going to turn into a bonding moment for the two of them where they could hug, say *I love you, man*, and sing campfire songs.

"Let her go if you can't possibly love her," Tyler told him. "Give her back her brother — you know you have the power to do it — and let her go."

"I can't let her go."

"Then I'll step in and help her," Tyler threatened

That came as another shock. Blake stared at his brother, wondering whether he'd been wrong to think Tyler would never step in and mess with his brother's woman. But the look on Tyler's face wasn't love; it was loyalty. He'd come across a woman who needed protection, and he felt compelled to give it to her. It was just who Tyler was.

"This isn't your business, Tyler."

Tyler was about to say something, but his mouth closed and he leaned back, his brows wrinkled, and his eyes flew up as if in shock. The way he was giving Blake the eye made Blake want to turn away. He absolutely didn't want to be analyzed.

"You're not saying... Do you love her, Blake?"

"No!" Blake practically shouted that word before he calmed himself down. "No, I don't love her. I just don't want to let her go yet."

"And you'll use a child to bribe her to stay with you, even when she can't stand the sight of you?" Tyler said.

That hit Blake below the belt.

"I can promise you that she wants me just as much as I want her."

"That isn't the impression that I got from her today. She seemed depressed, defeated, and out of options. Do you really want her to be with you because you're her last resort?"

Blake sat back and thought about his time with Jewell, and the months of agony without her. Yes, their time together had been short, but in their time apart he'd thought of no one but her. Yes, he'd had the opportunity to replace her immediately, but he hadn't felt even a twinge of desire to do so. After a week, he'd been stunned that he still felt the same way.

After three months, he'd decided to do something about the situation. If she was still on his mind, he'd told himself, he had to see this through to the end. And that's what was happening now.

"She and I will marry, Tyler. It's not as if that has to lock us together for life. But if I marry her, she'll easily get custody of her brother, and she'll be tied to me for as long as I see fit." Blake spoke with just enough arrogance to piss his brother off all over again.

But just when he thought Tyler was going to come unglued, his brother amazed him by cracking a smile.

"You're nothing but show right now — do you know that?" Tyler said, and laughed.

That laugh got underneath Blake's skin far more than the lecture his brother had been giving him.

"What in the hell are you talking about now, Tyler?"

"You know you actually care about this woman; you care about her far more than you'll admit. Are you afraid of telling *me* how you feel, or are you afraid to tell *her*?"

"I'm afraid of no one," Blake thundered. Fear wasn't an emotion he ever felt.

"Why not just date the woman properly, then, instead of continually buying her and making her feel cheap?"

Sheesh. Now his brother was channeling Max. "Jewell's the one who put herself into the situation she's in," Blake pointed out. "She *chose* to join an escort service."

"No she didn't. You know perfectly well that she had no choice. She'd do anything for her brother, just as I'd do anything it took for you or Byron."

"And I'll do anything to be with her." Blake didn't realize how much that revealed to his savvy brother.

"What does that mean?" Tyler asked him "You'll do anything to have sex with her?"

"I shouldn't say this even to you, but the sex is incredible. It's more than sex. It's something so powerful you couldn't possibly comprehend it, little brother."

"Just because it's great sex and more doesn't mean you have the right to take it when it's not offered freely."

"Believe me when I say that our sex life is no hardship on her," Blake said smugly.

"You're demanding marriage, Blake. Great sex will fade, and then you'll find yourself living with a woman who resents you."

"I don't think so. I've been with a lot of women in my lifetime and I've never had a connection like the one I share with Jewell. She knows this, too — she's just fighting against her feelings.

"Do you really believe this?" Tyler asked.

"I believe that we're meant to be together." Blake wanted to show that he wasn't trying to hurt Jewell, that he did feel something, even if he was unsure of exactly what that was. But he wasn't sure how.

"I'll be watching you, Blake," Tyler informed him.

"I wouldn't have it any other way," Blake said, and he stood up.

Tyler rose as well and Blake walked around his desk. "Don't screw this up," Tyler said.

"We've always trusted each other, Tyler. Don't lose your faith in me now." Blake shook his brother's hand.

Tyler stepped back and looked at Blake again, making him feel as if he were beneath a microscope, and then, without another word, Tyler left the office and Blake sat back down and turned his chair away from his open door.

Closing his eyes, he thought about the previous night with Jewell. It was perfect, as usual, but it wasn't enough, even though they'd made love for hours on end. With her it was never enough.

Groaning, he shifted in his seat as his body hardened. He could practically smell her, taste her on his tongue. Only this woman had ever been able to make him hard at just a single thought. That wasn't something to let go of.

But what if Jewell really was afraid of him? No, that wasn't possible. He was demanding, to be sure, and he expected a certain amount of respect from her, but he was also willing to offer her everything she could ever possibly desire. They had something, and she knew it. She didn't fear him — that was impossible. She just wanted to establish her independence.

He'd give Jewell a couple of days to think about what she truly wanted. That would do her some good. And he would once again be back on top. He wouldn't let this visit with Tyler sway him. Jewell was his — and only his.

CHAPTER FOURTEEN

"DAMMIT!"

Jewell looked down at the blood dripping from her finger and scurried over to the kitchen sink, where she washed the shallow wound before grabbing some paper towels and wrapping it so she could get to her bathroom without dripping blood through the apartment.

Her mood was less than perfect. It had been three days since Tyler had been to her apartment, three long days and longer nights without a single word from him about what was going to happen. This was her freaking life Blake was playing with.

Blake had told her he would give her a couple of days to think, and those couple of days had turned in to three. What the heck was going on? Had Tyler spoken to him? Was he going to back off? Was he giving up on her?

All it would take to find was a simple phone call, but as many times as she picked up her phone, she still hadn't managed to dial his number. What if the pot was on a low simmer, and she set it to boiling?

She'd certainly made phone calls over the past three days, but they hadn't been to Blake, and they'd gotten her nowhere. She felt she was on a first-name basis with the court clerks now. The children's services division hadn't been any help so far, and she was desperate to at least visit with Justin. But she needed permission and so far she wasn't getting it.

Maybe Blake knew all of this was happening, knew that if he waited her out, she'd cave and he'd get what he wanted. Of course he would. Tyler hadn't been able to help her as much as he'd probably hoped to, and now she wasn't even that afraid of marrying Blake. It wasn't on her bucket list, but her fear of losing Justin was greater than her fear of falling in love with a man who could never love her.

When Jewell couldn't stand being in the apartment a single minute longer without flipping out completely, she grabbed her coat and headed off to the elevator. To get away from phones would help her not make a call she was sure to regret.

Jewell found herself at a corner bar not far from her place, and she didn't hesitate to take up residence at one of the barstools.

"What can I get for you?"

"Something sweet and strong," she answered.

"Ah, you're having one of those days, huh?" asked the woman behind the bar.

"I'm having one of those weeks…or months…or maybe years," Jewell replied as the woman mixed her drink.

"You know it's a bad day when the drinking starts at two in the afternoon," the woman replied, not unkindly. "Here ya go, sweetie. The first one is on the house."

Strangely, the bartender's kindness nearly undid Jewell.

"Thank you," she said as she accepted the tall, fruity drink and took a long swallow. "Oh, this is exactly what I needed. What's it called?"

"You probably don't want to know. But yeah, I think it has magical powers. Or maybe if you just drink enough of them, your head gets so fuzzy, it just feels like they have magical powers. I'm Tina, by the way," she said, and held out her hand.

"I'm Jewell," she responded, and the two women shook hands happily.

A group of young men came in, and the bartender was then busy for the next few minutes as she checked their IDs and got their drinks. One of the kids, who couldn't be more than a few months over twenty-one, came and sat by her.

"Can I buy your next drink?" he asked with a hopeful smile.

"Trust me, you're going to be much better off buying it for one of the young ladies over there," Jewell said with a smile as she pointed to a group of what looked like college girls in the corner.

"Nah, the girls my age are too shallow," he said with a wink as he motioned for Tina to come over to them. "Can I get another drink for the lady?"

Tina smiled as she looked at Jewell, who shrugged her shoulders. She was surprised to see her first drink was finished. Then another was being set in front of her, and when that one was gone, she found herself laughing with the whole group of boys, who she learned were attending the University of Washington.

She stopped her drinks after the third one, knowing she didn't want to end up doing something foolish, but when three hours passed and she felt immeasurably better, she thanked the boys and Tina, and then decided it was time to go home. She would much rather eat food at her own place than deep-fried bar food.

Her companions lodged protests, but they didn't hassle her too much when she left and made her way back down the streets in a much better mood than she'd been when she first set out on this minor adventure. That good mood immediately vanished when she walked in her front door and heard laughter coming from the sitting room.

Her stomach clenched when a male voice piped in. Her part-time housekeeper wasn't alone, and though Jewell could pretend the person with Elsa was anyone other than Blake, she knew beyond a doubt he was there. Of course he could disappear for days on end and then show up whenever he felt like it. It was his apartment, after all; he seemed to own everything and everyone.

When she stopped in the doorway and saw Blake with a smile on his normally stern face, laughing at something Elsa had said, she felt an odd surge of jealousy. That was ridiculous. If he wanted to run off with her housekeeper, a woman he'd hired, that would save her a lot of hassle. She should leave them to their fun, just walk away in relief.

That isn't what she did, of course. Instead, she took another step forward.

Jewell's eyes were drawn to the laugh lines next to his eyes as his face opened up, making him so much more human. He was wearing a pair of jeans that hugged his thighs to perfection, and a shirt that seemed molded to his sculpted chest.

Her stomach clenched with raw need, and her head started to spin a bit. When she tried to take another step, she found herself gripping the doorjamb and holding on for dear life.

She was glad that neither Blake nor Elsa had noticed her yet, because it gave her a moment to compose her features, to pull herself together. She was really regretting her drinks, even if she was no longer feeling their full effect.

When Blake's shoulders tensed and he turned his head only an inch in her direction, she knew he'd become aware of her presence. Maybe he had been the whole time. Maybe the flirting and the laughter had all been for her benefit. It seemed that everything Blake did was calculated, so why wouldn't this be as well?

There was no use hiding now, so she finally let go of the doorjamb and moved into the room, hoping her voice would sound normal when she was expected to speak.

"You're home sooner than I expected, Ms. Weston. I haven't begun dinner yet," Elsa said, and she stood up.

"It's fine, Elsa. I'm not very hungry," Jewell replied.

"Oh, pish posh. I'm sure you're starving after being out all afternoon. Time just got away from me. Mr. Knight is very entertaining company," Elsa said as she started to leave the room.

Jewell gritted her teeth at the "company" comment. It had looked like Elsa and Blake were enjoying each other's company a little too well, she thought snidely, but she was proud of herself for not speaking those thoughts aloud. It was also stupid to let it affect her. Hadn't she told him to give her Justin and find another woman to help close his big business deal? Maybe he was doing just that.

"I'm sorry for keeping you, Elsa, but I appreciate that you didn't leave me to sit here all alone," Blake told her, his voice positively dripping honey and making Jewell grind her teeth together.

"Don't let me interrupt you guys," Jewell said. "I really need to go take a shower anyway."

"I'll have dinner ready in half an hour," Elsa said. The housekeeper was obviously beginning to feel the tension in the room, and desperately eager to escape — which was exactly what Jewell wanted to do herself. "You'll be staying, won't you, Mr. Knight?"

"Yes, I'd love to have dinner here, Elsa."

And with that, Elsa scampered away, leaving Jewell standing there. And just her luck — Blake caught her eyes and held on with that powerful gaze of his. She didn't know what to do or say first. There was so much on her mind, so many unanswered questions.

Had Tyler really spoken to him? Was Blake going to give up on this crazy notion that they should get married? If he was going to give up on that, was he also done with the affair? And what about Justin?

Instead of acting on her urges to ask him anything, Jewell quickly hightailed it. She rushed to her bedroom, then shut and locked the door, and leaned against it. After catching her breath, she went into the bathroom and took an extra-long shower.

So what if she spritzed herself with superexpensive scented body oil? She was only continuing the routine she'd started since finding the stuff in the room. There was no thought of pleasing Blake, she assured herself. That was the last thing she was interested in doing this evening.

Finally emerging from the bathroom, she followed the sound of laughter once again and found Blake and Elsa in the kitchen preparing dinner together. And once again, the sight stopped her in her tracks. Blake wasn't normally so helpful. Maybe something really was going on between him and the housekeeper. Did Elsa keep house for him too? She was here only a couple of times a week…

"Do you need me to do anything?" Jewell asked as she joined them.

"It's actually almost ready. Mr. Knight was a terrific help. He prepared the beef medallions while I worked on the vegetables and dessert," Elsa said as she checked the oven. Whatever they'd made smelled terrific, and Jewell's stomach gave a quiet growl of appreciation.

A few minutes later, the meal was complete and Elsa insisted that Jewell sit. When Blake chose to sit not across from Jewell but beside her at the end of the table, she squirmed slightly at his close presence.

Elsa put the plates down on the table, and Jewell's first taste was an explosion of flavors on her tongue. When she turned to thank Elsa, she discovered that the woman was already gone. So Jewell turned her attention back to her food. As she nibbled away, and the silence began to grow oppressive, she couldn't help but think of other meals she'd shared with Blake back at his apartment. More than one had ended with her on the table as dessert for Blake.

The sad part was that she wouldn't mind reenacting a few of those moments here and now. The thought killed her appetite. Hoping that Blake wouldn't notice and maybe guess why she was so rattled, she moved food around on her plate.

He noticed. "You've lost weight, Jewell. Please don't let my presence stop you from eating. You obviously need the calories."

When she didn't look up, she heard movement and

then his fingers were beneath her chin, tilting it up to force their eyes to meet.

"I think I may have a bug or something," she said. It was the only excuse she could think of on the spur of the moment.

"Do lies roll so easily off your tongue that you don't even notice it when you tell them now?" he asked her.

"I think that was very rude," she replied.

"I think you get offended far too easily, Jewell."

"Maybe because I just don't know what to expect next from you." That was about as honest as it got for her.

"I've laid my cards out on the table, Jewell. If I haven't told you that I want something, I'm not expecting it."

"Did you talk to Tyler?" she blurted out. She couldn't take the waiting anymore.

Blake said nothing for a few heartbeats, showed no expression, and then he got up from the table and she wondered if he was going to simply leave without saying a word. She didn't know what she would do if that happened.

He grabbed dessert from the sideboard and sat back down with a smile. "I can think of other more tasty desserts," he said.

"Is that what you want, Blake — me on the table?"

"I always want you, Jewell," he said, but he didn't lean forward, didn't capture her lips, didn't follow through on his words.

"Don't you own me, Blake? Isn't that what you paid for?" Damn. Her voice was just a little too breathless to carry off the sarcasm she hoped to infuse into her words.

"There's plenty of time for me to sample your body, Jewell," he said as he released her gaze and then set one piece of pie on her plate and one on his own. He started digging in, leaving her mouth hanging open.

She'd given him the green light and he hadn't taken it. Why?

"Please just tell me if you spoke with your brother," she said.

"I don't want to have that discussion right now," he replied calmly.

"Why? Is this just another way for you to assert your control?"

"Maybe," he replied before sighing. "Look, I'm not demanding answers from you tonight, am I? I asked you to marry me, and I'm not quizzing you on that, so you can show me the same respect and not quiz me."

"Who are you and what have you done with Blake Knight?"

"You know who I am — who I've always been. I'm the man who wants you." Blake rose and looked down at her with one of his patented unreadable expressions. "Elsa's dinner was wonderful, Jewell. Your company was even better." And he headed toward the front door.

She had no idea what to think now. Was this a bluff? Did he want her to beg him to stay? The front door opened, and before she could think, let alone talk, he was out the door and it was closing behind him.

She stood next to the table stunned. He hadn't tried to kiss her; hell, he'd barely touched her. He also hadn't answered a single question she'd thrown at him. What did it all mean? After disappearing for three days, he'd showed up unexpectedly, talked about trivial things, and walked away again.

And she still had no answers.

CHAPTER FIFTEEN

SILENCE.

That's what Jewell experienced for the next few days after Blake's strange dinner visit and even stranger exit. After three days passed and she heard not a single word from him, she began to wonder if he'd finally decided that one night of great sex more than a week ago was enough. But he was more playing a game with her, trying to drive her insane. He would make her so crazy she would just collapse in a puddle at his feet and beg to do his bidding.

Jewell woke up each morning with her body tense but this morning something was really off. She could feel it, and she was terrified of opening her eyes. Lately, she'd so often been delighted to wake up, to leave behind the disturbing dreams that seemed to fill her mind every night, but this morning she wished she were still asleep, because she knew she wasn't alone.

"You might as well open your eyes, Jewell. I can tell you're awake."

Her body went instantly from tense to a stiff as a board. That voice had been in her dreams, in her thoughts, every minute of every day for months — ever since she'd met him.

She kept her eyes closed and shifted restlessly on the bed, but after a minute she gave up and spoke. "What are you doing here, Blake?"

"I have given you enough time to think, Jewell. More than enough. I'm done waiting."

Jewell finally opened her eyes and found him leaning over her.

"You can't just walk into somebody's home, especially their bedroom, while they are sleeping," she said. She was sure she looked terrible, with her hair a mess and dark circles under her eyes. This wasn't exactly the time to entertain company.

"But I own this apartment, Jewell."

"You don't own me," she retorted before clapping her hand over her mouth. Of course he did, and he didn't hesitate to remind her of that unhappy fact.

"You can say that all you want — but I do own you, Jewell," he whispered. "And you've even admitted it on occasion." Then, as if to prove his ownership, he slipped his hand beneath her covers and cupped her breast on the outside of her nightshirt.

Her traitorous body instantly responded to him, her nipple hardening, her stomach quivering, and her breath hitching. And there was no hiding those reactions.

"Just because you can make my body respond, it doesn't mean that I want you."

Blake's pupils dilated. "I think that's exactly what it means, darling Jewell," he said. "You can either get up and come out with me for the day, or we can just spend it right here — in this nice warm bed."

While he spoke, he withdrew his hand from her breast, making her want to scream and tell him to put it right back where it had been, but then she felt his warm palm slip under her shirt and travel upward until his fingers were on her bare breast.

When he squeezed her nipple between his thumb and forefinger, she whimpered, much to her distress and shame. Yes, he turned her on, and yes, he knew it.

"You love my touch, Jewell. No matter how much you deny it, you can't fool me," he told her. He lifted her shirt without removing it and his mouth took the place his hand had just occupied.

She couldn't help but moan. She'd tried over and over to claim otherwise, but oh how she wanted him. She couldn't even hate him for it. When they both lapsed into silence, he stopped touching her and rose from the bed, then began to undo his shirt. She knew that if she said nothing, they'd end up making love, and her body was just screaming for sex.

So she was shocked when she spoke. "Let me shower, Blake. I'll be ready to leave in thirty minutes."

"Too bad," he said with a sigh.

He stepped closer and lifted her hand, placing it where his hardness was pulsing beneath his pants. She nearly changed her mind.

But somehow she found the strength to get out of bed and head to the bathroom. As the warm spray caressed her sensitive skin, she wished she had the courage to call him in so he could relieve the ache she was feeling. But she finished her shower alone, got dressed, and found Blake in the kitchen drinking coffee.

"Where are we going?" she asked, pouring herself a cup and taking a sip.

"To the marina."

"Why? What are we going to do there?"

"You'll see. I have plans," Blake told her.

After finishing her coffee, Jewell went with him to the front door. He took her jacket from the coat closet and helped her into it, then led her from the apartment.

He said nothing as the two of them stepped into the elevator, and then suddenly it was as if a dam had broken, because Jewell found herself pressed against the elevator wall, with Blake's body covering hers and his head descending.

The kiss he gave her left her knees weak. His hands traveled up and down her back, and her body melted underneath the possession. What had she been thinking when she turned down lovemaking in favor of going out?

The bell on the elevator chimed, and he stepped back and quickly helped her tug her clothes back into place, though the glow in her cheeks would make any onlooker aware that she was a woman who had just been thoroughly kissed. The two of them got off the elevator in silence, proceeded through the lobby of the apartment complex, and walked out onto the street, where Blake had a car waiting.

"To the marina, sir?" Max asked.

After Blake and Jewell climbed into the backseat, he lifted her hand to his mouth and feathered kisses across her knuckles, making her stomach twist.

Max said nothing; he didn't so much as look in the rearview mirror as Blake attempted to seduce Jewell right there in the car. Suddenly she was angry. This miserable man came and went as he pleased, left her feeling wanted and then unwanted, made sure she didn't know where she stood, and he still had the ability to make her pant for him in a matter of seconds.

It wasn't right and she didn't want to have anything to do with it. She tugged her firmly away and sat on both hands so he couldn't gain access to either of them.

"Hmm, playing hard to get?" he whispered in her ear, and then leaned down and warmed her neck with his hot breath.

"Maybe I don't appreciate you touching me," she said — what a ridiculously obvious lie!

"I think you enjoy me touching you anytime, anywhere," he countered, his hand now on her thigh and slowly traveling upward.

"You did pay for me, so I guess you bought the privilege," she said nastily, and he paused for a moment before leaning even closer.

"Yes, I did." Though she'd been the one to point it out, having him confirm it didn't make her feel any better. "Open your thighs, Jewell." That wasn't a request; it was a command. "If you want to be treated like a whore, I'm more than willing to oblige you."

Tears stung her eyes, but she turned to glare at him before she did as he asked. His expression showed nothing as he moved his hands up the inside of her jeans-clad leg, and then ran his finger on the outside of her core, sending shivers all through her.

"I can take you whenever I damn well feel like it. Don't forget that." He removed his hand and turned away from her.

He didn't touch her again while they traveled down to a part of the bay where only the richest of the rich stored their yachts. The car stopped and Max came around and opened the back door.

"Let's go," Blake said gruffly.

Jewell had no idea what he was thinking, but she suspected that she'd put him in a very bad mood. Good. She was hurting, so it was only fair that she'd spoiled his fun, too.

If only she really felt that way. They walked in silence to where the huge boats bobbed on the water. Jewell fought tears as she waited to see what would come next.

CHAPTER SIXTEEN

BLAKE WAS FURIOUS. He was trying to treat Jewell better and she wasn't allowing it. If she wanted to throw in his face that he owned her, then he damn well was going to show her exactly what he could do with his property. He knew he could try to handle this a bit differently, but for some reason he reverted back to the hard asshole she expected him to be, and he couldn't seem to stop it.

That thought made him even more furious. Here he was trying to be a good guy — he was taking her out on a freaking date! — and she wasn't being cooperative.

He'd been rock hard since the moment he walked into her bedroom and saw her lying there, her body restless, the blankets falling away, and her sleep shirt not offering much of a barrier to his view.

He wanted her, and yet he'd given her a choice on waiting to have sex. But the choice was out of her hands now. If she wanted him to be controlling, controlling was exactly what he would be. As much as she protested, maybe, just maybe, she liked having him take command.

Her world had been spinning out of control since she'd lost her mother, and maybe what she needed was someone to stop the spinning, someone to pull her from the whirlwind she was trapped in. Whatever the reason, she seemed to settle down only when he gave her no other choice.

None of that shaky pop psychologizing mattered at the moment, though. All that mattered was that he was hungry for her, and he'd had enough waiting. His brother had made him think, but Blake wasn't about to change who he was — not for his family and certainly not for this woman, a woman who made his world spin out of control too, and did it every time she was near.

"Wow!"

Blake stopped his internal rant when Jewell's feet stopped moving and he heard her exclamation.

"What?" he asked. He couldn't tell what had made her so excited.

"Are you really so used to this much wealth that you don't see what's right in front of you?"

Blake looked at the yacht gently bobbing at the dock in front of them. Was what she'd said true? Did he really not notice these things anymore? That wasn't something that pleased him. There'd never been a time when he was poor, but he still appreciated all he had. Or did he really? When it came down to it, was there any more excitement left in his life?

If there wasn't, there would be now. He decided it was time to create some. Instead of going to his own boat, he moved her toward the one she was admiring.

"Let me show you the inside," he said, once again taking

her hand as he helped her aboard the nearly two-hundred-foot vessel.

"I didn't know private boats were made this big. Does this belong to you, Blake?"

He decided not to answer that question yet. "Many people own large boats. They become a sort of second home. You can live on them if that's what you choose," he told her.

"Sort of like Tom Hanks in *Sleepless in Seattle*," she said with a nervous giggle.

"Well, his wasn't quite this size."

"Yeah, that's true." Her voice was hushed as they climbed on board.

He tried to see the boat through Jewell's widened eyes as they passed top-of-the-line furniture and exquisitely laid tables. Blake was more than ready to claim Jewell again. He rushed her through the boat and stepped inside what seemed to be the main stateroom.

She gasped in delight. The walls were mahogany; wide-open windows and gleaming glass doors led out to a private balcony. The ceiling was gilded; it was as if they were floating in a classic English country house. The room had in its center a huge four-poster bed that he was going to get her into — if he made it that far.

"Jewell…," he said, and she didn't hear him. "Jewell…," he said again and she turned, her face the picture of awe.

"Sorry. What?" she asked, looking around the room again.

Walking up to her, he placed his fingers beneath her chin and backed her against a built-in bookcase filled with rare books, books he'd love to explore at any other time.

"I'm going to peel your clothes away, piece by piece,

slowly and completely, and then I'm going to take you hard and fast. And then we'll start all over again and do it all night long. I can please you in ways no one else ever could."

"But…this…here?"

"Right here. Right now." Blake pressed body up against hers, letting her feel how ready he was to take her right this instant.

"This is your boat, isn't it?" She looked around nervously, as if finally realizing that the décor wasn't exactly his style.

"Why would you ask that? Are you afraid of being caught?"

"Yes," she said nervously, looking away from him over to the door he'd shut firmly behind them.

"That's part of the appeal," he told her, and his excitement built.

"Why are you doing this right now? Why here?"

"Because I can."

Jewell's eyes widened. His body pulsing with need, Blake grabbed her for a kiss she wouldn't soon forget. He knew he'd never get enough of this woman. And, surprisingly, he didn't want to.

CHAPTER SEVENTEEN

FIRE AND ICE. Jewell was frozen to the spot when Blake took her into his arms, but she was also burning up. His body was an exciting new world that she wanted to explore, wanted to know so much better than she already knew it. She couldn't resist this man, and she was tired of trying to.

The air weighed down on her lungs, and her entire body throbbed with desire. His power, her loss of control, the pure lust shining from his eyes should have disgusted her, should have filled her with fear. They hadn't. She was his.

After he pinned her against the bookshelves, all she could do was reach for him, desire him, crave him.

"This is why you'll eventually see things my way, Jewell. You are as powerless as I am to resist what is happening between us," he said before sinking his teeth into her shoulder, making her cry out in pain and pleasure.

"Stop talking," she panted. She was trying to get her brain to work and she couldn't. Had he just said he was powerless? Before she was able to focus on that, his hands smoothed down her backside and made her forget all about his words.

"Do you want to stop?" he asked, and she didn't know whether he was bluffing or not, but no, she didn't want to stop.

She might just perish if they even thought about it. She wouldn't say that, though. Instead, she slid her hand down between them and she cupped him, desperate to feel the raw power residing between his legs.

"You can keep silent all you want, Jewell. Your body talks plenty for you," he said with a laugh. That laugh turned into a gasp as her fingers squeezed his thick staff.

As he continued seducing her, her clothes began falling away. Her shirt was now lying on the floor, and her jeans a puddle at her feet, leaving her standing before him in only the thin lace of her panties.

He stepped back and gazed reverently at her. "You are so unbelievably gorgeous."

She wanted to repeat those words to him as he unbuttoned his shirt and let it slide downward, revealing his magnificent chest. Then he undid his belt and the top button on his pants, and her mouth watered in anticipation of seeing him in all his naked glory. But he didn't undo any more buttons, making her want to scream.

"Lie down on the bed," he demanded. "Leave your panties on, but spread your legs for me."

"No."

His brows rose at her refusal.

"You finish undressing first, Blake."

"That isn't how this works, Jewell. You do what I say," he told her, his eyes burning.

"Maybe I want *you* to do what *I* say," she replied. Her own boldness stunned her.

His lips turned up. "I love it when you fight me, Jewell," he said, then he moved toward her with lightning speed, spun her around, and trapped her hands behind her back.

"Let go," she told him fiercely. She knew better than to challenge him, but it wasn't fear she was feeling anymore; it was pure, unadulterated excitement.

She heard the low whoosh of his belt slipping through the loops of his pants, and then she felt him wrap the soft leather around her wrists.

And *now* she felt a sliver of fear, too. "What are you doing, Blake?"

"Whatever I want," he whispered into her ear. He pushed her forward, making her knees come in contact with the bed. It was only seconds before he lifted her up, leaving her derrière high in the air, her face on the bed, and her hands secured tightly behind her back.

He caressed her backside with his hands, then slipped a finger inside the edge of her panties and felt her undeniable wetness, wetness proving how turned on she truly was.

"See, Jewell, you can lie with words all you want, but your body tells me exactly how much you enjoy this, exactly how much you want me."

Then his palm came down and she let out a shocked cry when he made contact with the tender flesh of her backside. The blow wasn't hard enough to hurt her; it was just enough to warm her skin and send a ripple of pleasure through her core.

"I've changed my mind. I don't want to take you hard and fast. I want to take you over and over again until you can't possibly stand another minute. I won't let you come until you're begging me to do so," he said, and he bent and gently nipped her buttock.

"I won't beg you," she said through gritted teeth. But would she be able to keep her word? She didn't know.

"Oh, you *will* beg me, Jewell. I guarantee it."

Before he was able to say anything more, they heard a pounding on the door, which instantly sent a cold chill through Jewell's body.

"Who's in there?" someone yelled. "Why is this door locked?" The pounding grew in volume.

"Go away," Blake shouted, his powerful voice enough to scare most people into doing exactly what he wanted.

"I watched you use a card to get on these docks. I thought this was your boat," Jewell gasped.

"I most certainly will not go away," the person called out. "This is private property — *my* boss's property — and you're trespassing. I'm calling the cops."

"You don't have permission to be on here?" Jewell said as she squirmed to try to get away, but Blake had his hand tightly on her hip.

"It belongs to a business associate who is selling it. It will be mine in one minute," Blake said, and he released her, though all she could do was roll onto her side. The belt around her hands didn't allow her to even cover herself.

"Let me out of this," she begged him, but Blake didn't seem to hear her.

He went over to his jacket and pulled out what appeared to be a checkbook. He wrote something furiously and went over to the door, not even bothering to put on a shirt or to button up his pants.

Opening the door, he blocked any view into the room. And Blake had to be a fearsome sight, because the man on the other side of the door took a quick step back. All Jewell could see were his feet through Blake's firmly planted legs.

"What in the hell do you think you're doing?" the man said, but his words weren't quite as loud as they had been while the door was closed. "This is private property," he said for the second time.

"This is my boat now. Get the hell off my property," Blake growled as he lifted the check he'd just written and slammed it against the stunned man's chest.

"I…what?" the man gasped.

"Call your boss." Without another word, Blake shut the door with a final click and bolted the lock, then turned and shot Jewell a look with so much heat that she wasn't sure how she didn't melt against the still-made bed.

"We won't be interrupted again," he said as he stalked back toward her.

"What if he doesn't want to sell his boat?" Jewell questioned.

"I told you I know the seller. I gave him more than he was asking. The boat is now mine."

"You can't just buy a boat without paperwork," she pointed out.

"I can."

Jewell was stunned.

"Where were we?" Blake said, hunger burning in his gaze.

"I'm not in the mood anymore," Jewell said; she was still in shock over the events of the past few minutes.

"Don't worry. I'll get you there."

With those words he undid the rest of the buttons on his pants, and let them fall to the floor. Apparently the interruption had done nothing to put a damper on his excitement — he sprang free, thick, long and hard, and Jewell felt a rush of liquid heat coat her quivering core.

She couldn't tear her gaze away from Blake as he walked back to the bed and stared down at her. Then, when he sat down, his erection so close to her face, she tried not to be affected, but it was impossible.

"Taste me, Jewell," he ordered her, and her throat tightened.

She wanted to taste him, wanted to feel his pleasure on her tongue.

He shifted his body and pulled her back up so she was on her knees, her mouth only inches from his gleaming shaft. When he brought her to his arousal, she didn't hesitate; she opened her lips to take him inside the recesses of her mouth.

"Yes, Jewell, just like that." He guided her head slowly up and down his pulsing thickness. She sucked his velvet skin and smiled around his manhood when she tasted the tang of his pleasure.

He supported her head with one hand so she didn't fall against him, while he reached around her throat with the other hand and let it glide downward until he was fondling her breast. He rubbed his palm against her aching nipple, then pinched it, making her cry out even as she sucked on him, and she took him deeper into her throat.

"Enough," he groaned, lifting her head. The sight of him wet with her saliva made her core throb.

"Please," she groaned.

"I thought you wouldn't beg."

She tensed at his words, irritated with herself for doing exactly what she'd said she wouldn't do. Well, she wouldn't do it again, no matter how much she wanted him buried deep inside her.

He looked at the stubbornness in her face and chuckled. "Ah, Jewell, you'll never win in a game of wills with me," he said, and she suspected that he was right.

But she said nothing. She wasn't willing to give him the satisfaction.

Then he moved off the bed and left her on her knees, with her ass arched in the air and her hands still trapped behind her back. The lights went out. She waited for his touch, but nothing happened, and she writhed on the bed, her core tight and needy, her breasts aching acutely as they rubbed against the blankets.

He was going to make her speak. She knew exactly what he was doing, and she held out for as long as she could before a frustrated sigh escaped her tightened throat.

"Okay, please touch me. Please, Blake." She knew that she was caving to his demands, but she also knew that it was a loss of dignity she could live with.

"Mmm, my pleasure," he murmured, before he pulled her backward, leaving her feet hanging off the bed, his hot breath suddenly on the sensitive flesh of her backside. His tongue flicked out and ran down one butt cheek and up the other before he spread her legs wide open and licked the outer lips of her pulsing core.

"More," she practically sobbed. The sensation of his rough tongue and hot breath was almost more than she could bear.

"Arch your back," he commanded her as he continued licking her most sensitive areas, and sucked the swollen bud of her womanhood into his mouth, making her cry out over and over again.

Just as she reached the edge of glory, he stopped.

"Please, Blake, don't stop now," she begged him, but to no avail. A sob ripped through her when she felt the bed shift, felt him draw his mouth away from where she needed it most.

"It's not yet time for you to be rewarded," he told her as he spread her thighs even wider and fit himself between them. The tip of his hardness was pressed to the outside of her core, and she wriggled in his grasp, trying to force him to enter her.

With a groan, Blake finally pushed forward and did as Jewell had bid him, sinking himself deep inside her with one powerful thrust that took her breath fully away.

He pulled back slowly and then thrust forward over and over again, not fast enough to allow her to come, but at a pace designed to keep her on the edge of the cliff. She pleaded with him to release the mass of tension that continued to build higher and higher within her, but he kept her hanging for what seemed like hours.

When she thought she couldn't stand it for another second, she felt him undo the knot on the belt that bound her hands, and then he was lying her down on her stomach. Still buried deep inside her, he lifted her hands and began massaging her numbed arms. She hadn't even realized they'd gone numb, she was so focused on the pleasure toward which he was leading her.

When he was finished massaging her, he withdrew from her body, making her cry out in protest, but then she was being flipped over and he was poised above her. He moved them both to the top of the bed, her head hitting the pillows.

He reached over and switched on the bedside lamp, then looked down at her, his eyes wild with passion. "I need to see the pleasure on your face when I make you come," he said, and he plunged back inside her.

Blake held nothing back any longer. He continued thrusting rapidly in and out, his face a figure of ecstasy, and she lost focus as her body released all the pressure that it had built up over the last couple of hours. In the throes of an orgasm more intense than anything she'd ever felt before, she didn't even try to hold back her scream.

She was barely maintaining consciousness when she heard his thundering groan and felt the pulsing of his manhood as he emptied himself into her, coating her slick walls with his passion.

Silence engulfed them as he pulled her against his chest and held her tightly. When her heart's erratic beat finally settled down, she nearly didn't hear his whispered words.

"It will only get better, Jewell. We're meant to be together."

CHAPTER EIGHTEEN

WHEN SHE EMERGED from sleep a few hours later, Jewell felt completely disoriented. Where in heaven's name was she? These sheets and these covers didn't feel like hers. Her adrenaline spiked, but then she felt Blake's body next to hers, felt his arm wrapped around her back, and felt his heartbeat beneath her hand.

Her eyes still closed, she savored the moment, fully letting her guard down as she enjoyed the comfort of being held. If only she could admit to Blake how much she needed this moment.

The sex had been wonderful — unbelievable, in fact — but this right now, right here was what she needed more than anything else. She needed to feel comforted by another person. By Blake. She shouldn't feel anything at all toward him, but her heart had made its choice.

Yes, he was demanding, and yes, he made no promises to her, but how could she not feel emotion toward this man who had changed her world so dramatically? Would it really be so bad to take his name, if that was even what he still wanted?

It would indeed be bad, because she had no doubt that if she spent too much time in this man's presence, she was going to fall in love with him, and that was something she couldn't afford to do. She was already too dependent on him.

When he disappeared for days — for more than half of the time, in fact, since he reappeared in her life — she'd felt unmotivated, almost listless. What would it be like if she were with him for months, or even years, and then he decided to toss her aside?

Could she be with him without giving him her whole heart? She doubted it. But what other choice did she have at this point? That was the fundamental question she needed to answer.

"Are you hungry?"

Jewell was jolted by the sound of Blake's voice, but she didn't know what to say, so she said nothing. Damn. Holding her tongue was becoming such a habit with her.

"Are you in a sex coma, Jewell?" he asked with a laugh as he turned her so she was now facing him.

She was afraid to open her eyes. Maybe if she stayed as she was for a little while longer, there wouldn't be any stress, no worries, nothing to upset the moment. She needed just a few more moments of no worry, to just accept the comfort of being in his arms.

"Ve haf vays, Fräulein Heston, of makink you talk," he said in an accent she'd never heard him use before. Was he actually joking around with her?

"I…uh…I'm awake," she finally said, letting her eyes slowly drift open.

"I think I'll enjoy this boat," he told her as he rubbed his hands up and down her back.

"I can't believe anyone would pay so much just to have sex," she blurted out, and then felt her cheeks turning red. Not only had he paid millions for his new boat so they could complete what they had started, but he'd also already paid a heck of a lot for her.

His mood lost its lightness. "Don't think about it, Jewell. Don't analyze it."

"How can I not? What in the world are we doing? Why would you want to help me? I just don't understand any of this." She'd laid out her vulnerability for him to see if only he cared to look.

"I explained it very well. You need help with your brother, and I need a wife for this business deal, so we're helping each other."

"You're are always so calm and determined. How can you make marriage a business deal?"

"Life is a business deal, so marriage can't be any different," he said, his voice firm.

"I don't feel like I have any other option, and that makes me almost despise you, you know."

He paused, his hands stilling on her naked skin, his face losing all expression and retreating behind the mask she was most familiar with.

"I don't need your love, Jewell."

This he had said before, but it still hurt. Even if she was saying things intending to wound him too, it still hurt.

"You just want my body, Blake."

"Yes." He didn't elaborate. Even though she hadn't asked him a question, he still answered.

"Don't forget that my little brother comes along with

me, Blake."

"I like kids."

"Have you ever even been around them?"

"I was a child once."

Jewell had a hard time believing that. It seemed more likely that he'd sprung from the womb full-grown. Okay, that was a bit ridiculous, but she couldn't imagine Blake smiling with dirt smeared on his cheeks, or running around playing cops and robbers. Yes, he worked on construction sites even now, but that was different than making mud pies or building forts.

"I don't think you know how to be carefree and go with the flow," she told him. "I don't think you even knew how to play games when you were a child. You're too hard, too set in your ways. You won't be good with Justin. You'll realize this eventually and then I'm the one who will pay the price."

He was quiet for so long that she figured her words had finally gotten through to him and he was deciding to break things off with her. Why did that cause such a pang inside her chest?

"Once I decide on a course of action, I don't change my mind, Jewell. I'm not letting you go, so don't waste your time thinking about it."

With that, he unwrapped his hands from her and stood up. Though she was exasperated with the man, she couldn't help but look at the magnificence of his naked behind, and she almost groaned when he pulled up his pants, covering up the prime view.

"I don't think we're ever going to agree on this," she said when he turned back toward her.

"It doesn't matter what you want, Jewell. It's about what

I want."

With that, he walked from the room. She gazed at his retreating form and sighed. What was worse than anything else at this moment was that she knew he was right.

It didn't matter at all what she wanted.

CHAPTER NINETEEN

"I'M GLAD YOU decided to come, Jewell."
Jewell looked at McKenzie Beaumont and attempted a smile. "I honestly don't know why I did. I guess if you call, I come," she replied softly. Jewell actually liked McKenzie. She had discovered in the months she'd gotten to know her employer that the woman wasn't nearly as hardened as Jewell had originally thought.

"You came because, for some strange reason, the two of us have made a connection. Anyway, I have a surprise for you," McKenzie said, and Jewell witnessed something she had never witnessed before with this woman — a sparkle in her eyes and an actual smile.

"Okay, you have me very curious now," Jewell replied.

"Come on in first and sit down." McKenzie ushered Jewell into the living room, done in beiges and reds. Jewell remembered McKenzie telling her once how a persons color choice could tell a lot about them. Was McKenzie looking for both peace in the beige and boldness in the red? Jewell didn't know. "I was able to arrange a visit with your brother. I told you I wanted to help you, and that's exactly what I'm trying to do," McKenzie told her.

"How?" Jewell exclaimed. Was this a joke?

"I have connections," McKenzie answered simply.

"But I've been getting the runaround for ages."

"Do you really want to talk about how it happened, or do you want to just be happy it happened?" McKenzie asked her.

"You're right. Where is he?" Jewell looked around.

"He should be here any minute," McKenzie told her, and Jewell's stomach knotted in anticipation. She was so afraid that Justin had thought she hadn't been trying to keep her promise to him.

" Thank you, Ms. Beaumont…"

McKenzie broke in. "That's the last time I want to hear you say 'Ms. Beaumont.' I'm McKenzie, and don't you forget that!"

"Then thank you, *McKenzie*. This means more to me than anything anyone has ever done for me," Jewell said, with a sheen of tears reflecting off her eyes. "I won't question you about who you had to bribe."

The look on McKenzie's face told Jewell that the woman might have actually done that, but the least Jewell knew the better.

"I told you that I have connections. Once I give my word, I keep it. That's all you need to know."

"I can live with that," Jewell said.

The two women had been sitting there for less than ten minutes when the doorbell rang and Jewell's stomach tightened once more.

"Sissy!" The excited cry rent the air, and Jewell's eyes instantly filled with tears as her little brother came barreling toward her.

"Ah, Bubby, it's so good to see you! I'm so sorry I haven't been able to keep my word," Jewell exclaimed a millisecond before he launched himself into her arms.

"I've missed you," he said with a sniffle, and he held on tight.

"And I've missed you so much. Oh, Justin, I am so, so sorry," she said again. How could she explain this all to her beloved little brother?

"It's okay. I just want to come home with you, though," he begged, leaning back and making her tears fall.

"I'm doing all I can to make that happen." She paused and decided to change the subject before she found herself making him more promises that she wasn't sure she could keep. "Oh my goodness, you've grown a foot since I've seen you last!"

"I've been doing what you said, Jewell, and eating my vegetables and being good. I want to live with you so much."

The boy clutched at his sister even more tightly. Nothing had ever felt so good for either of them.

"I'm working on it, Justin," she said. When he grunted, she loosened her own grip around him. "I love you so much."

"I love you too, Sissy. McKenzie has been visiting with me, and she told me that you are doing everything you can so we can be together."

Shocked, Jewell whipped her head around to where McKenzie was standing. The woman looked away, but Jewell had seen her cheeks color. It was as if McKenzie didn't want anyone to know that she had human kindness within her heart.

But wait. How had McKenzie been able to visit with Justin when Jewell couldn't? Jewell didn't know whether to feel anger over that, or relief because Justin hadn't been abandoned utterly. What was wrong with the court system!

"You've been going to see my brother?" Jewell asked as Justin released his hold on her and spotted the cookies McKenzie had been setting out.

"You weren't able to, and I know what he means to you," McKenzie said with a sadness in her voice that hinted at an untold story from her past.

"I appreciate it, McKenzie, more than I can say," Jewell told her, and she struggled with tears. Her happiness over such kindness to Justin won out over her ridiculous jealousy.

"I did what anyone would do. Now let's not discuss it," the woman said in her no-nonsense voice.

Before they could say anything more, they were interrupted again. Tyler walked into the room and headed straight for Jewell. "Hello, beautiful. I've missed you," he said before lifting her off the ground in a bone-crunching hug.

"Tyler? What are you doing here?" she asked when she was able to breathe again after his viselike grip.

"I'm here for the party. You know I can't turn a good one down," he said with a grin.

"Party? I didn't realize there was a party," Jewell said as she turned to look at McKenzie.

"I've invited a few people over. It's not a big deal," McKenzie said. Then the four of them made their way out back, where music was playing and about two dozen people were milling around.

"This is more than a few people," Jewell gasped, not knowing a single person there except for McKenzie, Tyler, and her little brother.

"The more people you have in your corner, the better, Jewell. See that man over there in the gray suit?"

Jewell nodded. He was currently laughing at something a beautiful brunette was saying to him.

"He's the district attorney here. And that man sitting over there in the black jacket is a judge. I told you I know people in high places. It will benefit you today to mingle," McKenzie told her.

"I don't know how to mingle," Jewell said in a panic as she watched her little brother run off to where a small group of children was swarming over a swing set. It didn't take him long at all to make new friends.

"It's a piece of cake and you know it. You just walk up to someone and start talking. If you remember that everyone loves to talk about themselves, you will get along fine. So ask about their families, work, hobbies, and interests, and you can have a full-on conversation while saying less than a dozen words yourself. The beauty of that is you get to know them well, and what they like, and they walk away thinking you're a wonderful conversationalist."

A man approached, and said, "Hello, McKenzie. Is this the woman you were telling me about?"

"Yes, Dr. Rice, this is Jewell Weston," McKenzie said. "How are the twins doing?"

"Oh, they're as active as ever. My wife doesn't know which day of the week it is on most days, she's so sleep deprived," he said with a genuine laugh.

"I can understand that," she said, laughing with him, though Jewell noticed the bleakness in the woman's eyes.

How much of what McKenzie put forth of herself was an act, and how much of it was real? The more Jewell was around this woman, the more she wanted to know the answer to that.

Jewell soon lost count of how many people she'd spoken to and how many stories she'd heard. But after a couple of hours, she felt more optimistic. She even had a job interview with the doctor; he had an opening in his accounting office. McKenzie had more than come through on what she'd promised Jewell. Maybe she could do this without Blake.

Jewell stepped inside the house to give herself a moment to breathe and to let her face rest — pasting a constant smile on it was too much like hard work — and then she felt as if she'd just been hit by a two-ton truck.

Standing there looking devastatingly handsome was Blake. Yes, she'd seen him only two days before, but neither of them been in contact after their argument on the boat, and she wasn't ready to see him yet.

But for that matter, how did McKenzie know Tyler? Jewell had been so shocked to see him, she hadn't questioned his relationship with her boss. Before Jewell could say a word, Justin bolted right past her and ran straight up to Blake. With a gigantic smile on his little face, the boy held out his arms and rushed in for a hug.

"Blake! I didn't know you were coming," Justin cried as Blake caught him in his arms.

Blake's smile was as wide as Justin's. "I wouldn't miss out on hanging with you, buddy," he said, leaving Jewell standing there stunned.

"How do you know my brother?" she demanded.

"We've spent some time together," Blake told her with

a shrug.

"When have you spent time together? And why wouldn't you have told me about it?"

"You never asked me," Blake replied.

She was seething, but she didn't want Justin to see it, since her brother obviously cared about the object of her wrath.

"You're not leaving any time soon, are you, Blake?" Justin broke in.

"Nope. I'll be here for a while," Blake replied. "Why?"

"I'm just going to go to the bathroom and then my new friends are waiting for me," Justin said before dashing off.

Jewell stayed silent until she heard the bathroom door slam shut. "It seems that everyone has been spending time with Justin, and no one felt the need to tell me about it," she said between clenched teeth.

"At first I wanted to make sure you were telling me the truth about him. I don't like women who lie," he said easily, not at all affected by her rage.

"And then later?" she questioned bitterly.

"It never came up," he said as he moved toward her.

"Anything that has to do with Justin is my business, and you know damn well I should have been told."

"I've been working with McKenzie to help you. We've actually both become attached to the boy," Blake said, stopping a few feet away from her.

"Attached?" she gasped. "Justin means the world to me. Enough to do all of this," she said as she held out her hands. "Please don't use him as nothing more than a pawn in a game you are the only one who knows the rules to."

If begging is what it took, she would resort to it, but she hated both herself and Blake for making her sink even more into this person she didn't want to be.

"It may have started out that way, Jewell, but I have feelings for the boy. I don't want to see him in the system. McKenzie feels the same way. And whether you believe it or not, I have feelings for you," he said, his eyes boring into hers.

"I don't believe you," she told him, looking away from the power of his eyes.

Blake paused. This was where he told her that her feelings didn't matter, right? Of course it was. This was where he went back to being the hard bastard she hated. But instead, he surprised her.

"You will." He said nothing more, but there was so much assurance in his tone, she thought he might be right. What if this man of steel actually did have other emotions locked deep down inside besides greed and desire?

"Why are we both here?"

"I don't understand the question," he said.

"When McKenzie called me, I thought she just wanted to speak to me, but why this party? Why this elaborate setup? I wish I just knew more of what everyone was thinking or doing. I truly don't understand any of this."

"Why do you think any of us do anything we do, Jewell?" He turned the question around on her.

"I think that you're bored," she said with a frustrated sigh.

His eyebrows rose as she spoke and he looked… confused. That wasn't what she was expecting at all. He wasn't acting in a way that she could read. She almost wished for the ice man she'd originally met to remake his appearance, because at least then she'd know exactly what to expect.

"If you'd let down your guard, Jewell, you would see that I'm not a monster."

"I need to visit with my brother." She turned and walked away from Blake. If she began to think that he actually cared about her, she wouldn't be able to fight him anymore.

She hadn't gone far when she ran right into Tyler. "Where are you off to in such a hurry?" he asked with a laugh before looking up and spotting his brother who quickly approached.

"I'm thirsty," she said as she tried to figure out how to get around Tyler without seeming too rude.

"I'm sure you're after a conversation with my brother," he said, placing his arm around her waist and turning her around to face Blake.

Blake looked pointedly at the fingers Tyler had on her side and sent his brother a look Jewell couldn't interpret. "I don't appreciate your sense of humor, Tyler," he said.

"Ah, I think you really need to lighten up, brother dearest." Tyler didn't free Jewell from his hold.

"I can think of a few ways to loosen up, and they all end with you picking yourself up off the ground," Blake said in a faux-pleasant tone.

"Do you really think, after all these years, that you frighten me?" Tyler let out a hearty guffaw.

"Don't mistake my love for you as weakness," Blake warned him.

"Love isn't a weakness," Tyler told him.

"It sure as hell was for our father," Blake retorted.

That one sentence seemed to suck all the oxygen from the area. Tyler's arm tightened around her as his muscles locked up and he sent Blake a glare. "There's no reason to bring that up right now, Blake," he said grimly.

"Then don't make asinine statements," Blake replied.

"Why in the hell do you always have to act so cold?" Tyler asked him. "I know who you are. Why can't you let other people see the man I idolize?"

"I don't know what you're talking about." Blake shifted, his anger instantly draining away.

"You know what I'm talking about, Blake. You aren't a monster, but you try so hard to act like one that people believe that's what you are."

Jewell had a feeling that both of them had forgotten she was even standing there with them.

"Ah, my brother, how I have you fooled," Blake said. "Yes, I care about a few things, but you have to have a conscience to care what others think about you."

Here was the man Jewell had been hoping would remake an appearance, but now that he had, she wanted him to go away.

"You have a conscience, Blake. It's just buried down deep. With very little effort you could find it again, sweep the cobwebs from it and show the world what you have shown to both me and Byron — not that Byron is acting any better than you are right now," Tyler said with a frustrated sigh.

"I'll consider what you've said," Blake told his brother, and Jewell knew he was done speaking about himself.

"I think I'm going to take Jewell to get that drink now," Tyler said, and he turned and led her away before Blake was able to say another word.

"You know this is going to really piss him off, don't you?" Jewell asked Tyler.

"Yes, I know, but I can't help but do my damnedest to

get underneath his skin," Tyler said as they reached the bar set up in one corner of the yard.

"You're not the one who will have to deal with his anger," Jewell said, but she couldn't find the energy to be upset with Tyler. He was just too sweet to her.

"Jewell, you have to come to grips with your own power as a woman. You are beautiful, kind, smart, and funny. You could easily have the old boy wrapped around your finger if only you tried." Tyler handed her a soda and grabbed a beer for himself.

"I think you way overestimate my abilities," Jewell told him.

"I am watching you blossom even as we speak."

"How can I blossom when I can't even find the sun?" she asked lightly. But she'd never felt anything more true.

"The sun is there, I promise you. Don't give up, okay. Promise me you won't," he said as he placed his hand on her shoulder and forced her to look into his eyes.

"I'll never give up. I can't. I have my brother to think about," she told him. And she was grateful, because without Justin, she probably would have given up a long time ago.

For the next couple of hours, Jewell avoided being alone with Blake, but she couldn't avoid his gaze, which followed her everywhere she went. She also couldn't avoid her brother's obvious love for the man. Justin grew giddy with excitement at the smallest amount of attention Blake decided to bestow on him.

Jewell's life seemed to become more and more complicated by the minute, and as the party wrapped up and it came time for Justin to return to his foster home, she felt even more unsure of what was coming next than she had even the day before.

Tears filled her eyes as she told Justin goodbye and watched him be driven away. And then she turned to find Blake right behind her. She couldn't spar with him right now. — she was just too drained.

"I hope you enjoyed your visit with Justin," he said.

Since she was on the verge of tears, she simply nodded and turned away so Blake couldn't see the rush of emotions trying to make themselves known.

"He looked happier than I've seen him in a while. I can see how much you mean to him," Blake said as he lifted a hand and moved a piece of hair from her face to behind her ear. The tender gesture just about threw her over the edge.

"We are all we have anymore — just the two of us," she finally said, her voice quiet.

"That's not true, Jewell. I'm standing right here."

"You're also not real, Blake," she said, hugging her arms across her body. She felt cold, so cold inside, after all the upheavals of the day.

"I'm very real, Jewell," he said, and then to prove that to her, he pulled her into his arms and kissed away any protests she might have.

She was locked tightly in his embrace while his lips caressed hers, and though she tried to keep her distance, tried not to let him in, the feel of his tongue on her lip, the feel of his body pressing against hers was more than she could bear.

She melted against him, and for a few brief moments, her worries evaporated, and she let go of the pain and anguish that seemed to be the principal components of her life now. When she was ready for him to carry her off into the nearest private space, he pulled back, placing his hands on her shoulders to steady her while she opened her eyes.

"I will see you tomorrow, Jewell."

Before she could say anything, he turned and walked away. She was left standing there in shock, and then anger, and then a deep sadness. The man kept doing the same thing, leaving her hanging and walking away.

Jewell managed to make it home, but she didn't make it far once she did. She collapsed on the nearest couch, where she finally cried herself to sleep.

CHAPTER TWENTY

JEWELL STUMBLED INTO her bathroom and glared at the image staring back at her from the mirror. "This is not who you are," she lectured herself. You've been through worse in life, and you will not let anything get in the way of your progress. Why in the world are you allowing one person to affect your emotions in this ridiculous way? Well, you're going to stop right this minute."

After her face — sadly, she looked only marginally better now — she went off to the kitchen and began her caffeine-centric morning ritual. Why was it such a chore to wake up, no matter how much sleep a person got?

After she'd downed her second cup of nature's perfect beverage, she heard a stomach-tightening knock. She could think of only two or three people who might be on the other side of her front door, and at the moment she wasn't in the mood to see anyone.

When the knocking sounded again, this time with a fierce *rat-a-ta-a-tat*, she knew it would do her no good to pretend she wasn't home. Peering through the peephole, she spotted Blake leaning closer and wearing a beaming smile. The jerk must have known she was looking out at him, and he was clearly enjoying the shock factor. At least he hadn't followed his usual M.O. and just barged in.

But they were on a merry-go-round, and she wasn't quite sure at this point when she was going to be thrown off. But if she wanted her final payment for services rendered, she couldn't worry about how she was feeling, could she?

Of course not.

"Can we do this later, Blake? I'm not awake enough to go rounds with you right now," she said through the door.

"Sorry, but no. I don't feel like leaving, Jewell."

"Then I guess you can stand out there looking foolish until I wake up."

"I have all day. As a matter of fact, I have no plans for the next few days."

"Don't you get tired of being told your presence isn't welcome?" she asked.

"Actually, it does get a bit wearing at times," he said more quietly.

Jewell had to strain to hear him through the door. The honesty in his voice — so rare from a guy who generally seemed to speak in only two registers, arrogance and sarcasm — amazed and affected her.

"Well, if you would listen to me, then I wouldn't feel the need to say such things," she told him.

"I'm trying to listen to you, and I'm trying to talk to you. You're the one who continues to turn all of our conversations into a fight."

That surprised her enough into opening up the door.

She gazed out at him, and when he didn't try to rush forward and invade her space, she gained a measure of respect for him. She didn't know what to say next and instead just found herself standing there and staring.

"May I come in, Jewell?" he asked.

"Fine. It's your place," she said grudgingly.

"Yes, it is, Jewell, but I'm trying to give you options."

"Why?"

"Because I want this to be mutually beneficial for both of us."

Another big surprise! "I need more coffee," she told him, and then shut her door behind him and led him into the kitchen.

"I spoke with Tyler after the party," Blake said, but he didn't continue.

"And what did the two of you talk about?" she finally asked.

Blake paused and a rueful grimace on his lips. "He told me I need to quit acting like an ass."

Jewell waited and when he again refused to elaborate, she let out an exasperated breath. "If you're going to just give these short answers, we'll be here all day."

"That's the plan," he said with the friendliest smile she'd ever seen him wear.

"Does Blake Knight have a twin — a good one?" She didn't know what to think of this man. He seemed almost…carefree. Yes, when she'd been around him recently, he'd been smiling more and more, but still, this person before her seemed like a completely new man.

"Can't a person change?"

"It doesn't happen very often."

"I'm trying, Jewell. I've decided it's better to listen when more than one person is telling me that the same old Blake isn't giving 'customer satisfaction,'" he replied, and he took her hand in his.

Jewell's head was spinning as he caressed her knuckles. "I…uh…I don't know what to think right now." She tugged on her hand, but he wasn't letting go.

"You don't always have to think, Jewell. Not everything has to be black and white, and sometimes it's simply better to trust your gut. We can't predict what will happen every minute of every day, but we can learn to roll with the changes."

"I'm sorry, but I don't trust you or this new you that you're presenting. Is that honest enough for you?"

"I can see why. Want to know what I did yesterday?" he asked, his eyes sparkling with excitement.

"I'm not sure I want to know," she replied, but her lips turned up just the slightest. It was hard not to be affected by his good mood.

"I'll tell you anyway," he said before pausing. "I bought a house."

"But you just bought that gigantic yacht! Anyway, you already have a place."

He decided not to tell her that he now owned *two* gigantic yachts; the house was a more important topic. "You're the one who told me there would be a child living with us."

"You bought a house with Justin and me in mind?" she asked as she was thrown off balance again.

"That's why I've been gone so much these past couple of weeks. I had to find the right place. This thing between us is on a track and there's no getting off it, so you might as well just accept it. It's fate."

"But…I…I'm confused. You run hot and then cold and you make these demands, and then you turn around and ask my opinion. I can't keep up with you, Blake."

"I've never pretended to perfect, Jewell. And I've never wanted to be in a relationship. Not a real one, at least. But we both have problems, and we can help each other with those problems. Will it be perfect? No, it won't, but who has a perfect life?"

"I've seen lots of shining examples of perfect lives," she told him.

"Blockbuster movies don't count, Jewell. In real life, people have their imperfections. Just one or two," he said with a chuckle.

"You're admitting that you aren't perfect, Blake?"

"I'm as close to perfection as it gets," he said, leaning back with a cocky grin.

"Ugh! You have too much self-confidence," she told him.

"Why shouldn't I? I know who I am and I know what I want. I always get it."

"Yeah. Yeah. I get it. You're the cat's meow," she said, trying to keep a straight face, but not succeeding.

"Again, I tell you that not everything is always black and white, Jewell," he said and she knew there was a story behind these words.

"If you expect me to do something I feel is wrong, then you have to give me a reason to do it, Blake."

He paused for a long moment before he spoke. "Isn't getting your brother back reason enough to do something you're uncomfortable with doing?"

"Yes. Of course Justin is worth anything and everything. But you want me to lock myself to you legally. And still you're not telling me why."

"For the business deal," he said.

"Yes, I can see you need to get married, but what I can't figure out is why you've chosen me."

"We have a connection. If I'm to give up my prized bachelor status, then I want to do it with someone I can stand to share a house with."

"I don't believe you."

Again, he paused for a long moment, and when he began speaking, Jewell's jaw dropped and she didn't think she'd ever be the same again.

CHAPTER TWENTY-ONE

IT WAS TIME to tell Jewell about his family. Blake knew that if he didn't do something drastic, he'd lose her in two weeks' time.

Though there was nothing she wouldn't do for her brother, she somehow knew that he wouldn't actually keep Justin from her if it came down to it. So he needed to give a piece of himself up, or else he was going to find himself without her.

He was thankful to his brother for talking to him, thankful he had actually listened to Tyler. He was so used to getting what he wanted no matter what he had to do to get it, he'd forgotten the basic rule that you get more with honey than with vinegar.

"You know that my family is incredibly messed up, right?"

She looked at him warily. "I know there's a story to be told," she said.

"I grew up wealthy. My father was a very rich man, and my mother…well, my mother was a gold-digging bitch."

Jewell's eyes popped open wide. "Surely, she couldn't have been that horrible," she said.

"What do you think of, Jewell, when you hear the word *mother*? Whatever adjectives you'll think of can't be used to describe that woman. She was vain, egotistical, and out to get whatever she could." Blake didn't feel even a glimmer of emotion — unless contempt counted — when he was describing the woman who had birthed him.

"Is that why you're so cold, Blake?"

"That's part of it."

"Byron and I remember it all vividly — all the fights, all the underhanded things our mother did, and the whipped man our father had become. She couldn't leave him and walk away with the money because she'd signed an unbreakable prenup. Sure, she could have gotten a lot of money for child support, but it wouldn't have been enough to cover the lifestyle that she'd grown accustomed to, and she didn't want us. She liked that we had a nanny, that she didn't have to deal with us. We barely even saw her, let alone communicated with her. Tyler was too young to be affected by her attitude and her actions, but Byron and I remember her very well."

"Lots of children have less than wonderful parents," Jewell pointed out. "But they don't take that as an excuse to treat everyone around them as nothing more than garbage beneath their feet."

"I agree, but how many children watch their parents die right before their eyes?"

"Wait! What do you mean?"

When Jewell took his hand, he was more than aware of it, even if he didn't think she realized that she was doing it, that she was trying to comfort him. It was a start, a start that he would take.

"My mother decided she didn't want to be with my father any longer. And she didn't want anything to do with my brothers and me. So she hatched a plan to have my father killed. Because her sons were nothing to her, she wasn't worried about any fallout. If we got hurt or even killed in the shuffle, then so be it." His voice sounded dead as he told her that.

"That's insane. There's no possible way anything like that could happen," Jewell exclaimed, her fingers tightening on his hand.

"It did happen, Jewell. I told you the world isn't always black and white and people aren't always who they are supposed to be."

"What happened?"

"My mother was seeing a man and told him that if he killed her husband, she would marry him and share all her wealth with him. Apparently the man she was seeing knew she was as big a liar with him as she was with my father. He found out somehow that her ultimate plan was to play the victim, throw him to the cops, and run off into the sunset with all her many millions of dollars. Her lover told her he was going along with her plan, but the entire time, he was making his own plans."

"What plans?" Jewell exclaimed.

A distant, lost look entered Blake's eyes when he told Jewell about the night that had changed him forever. "I was ten years old when it happened. My brothers and I were watching an animated movie in the family room when we heard shouting coming from the hallway. We just ignored the noise —it wasn't abnormal to hear raised voices in our house and continued watching our cartoon."

"But this shouting was different," Jewell said when Blake paused too long.

"Yes, this shouting was different. These two men suddenly came into the room, and they were pushing my parents ahead of them. Before we even knew what was going on, they had my parents each tied up to a chair and then they bound us, and set us on the couch. I'll never forget the look in my mother's eyes. They were practically glowing with excitement. I thought it had to be some sort of game, because she looked anything but worried."

"How could she not be worried? These men had bound her up," Jewell pointed out.

"Yes, but you see, that was all part of the plan. She couldn't get away unscathed, or the cops would never buy her story. My mother's sick and twisted plan was for her boyfriend to 'rape' her and kill her husband. And this plan included us, you see, because we had to be witnesses to what happened, so when the cops asked, we could say the men hurt her, too," Blake said with a disgusted snort.

He could see the horror in Jewell's eyes, and she dug her fingernails into his hand. She didn't realize how hard she was holding on to him. Strangely enough, the pain in his hand stabilized him enough to continue speaking.

"Things obviously didn't go according to my mother's plans. She figured that out pretty soon, and that's when I saw the panic enter her eyes. Her boyfriend told her he knew she was a sadistic bitch out to get anything she could. He then told my father her entire plot. My dad was weak and he started sobbing, begging the men to spare his life. Of course, they were very amused. They began beating him, and his blood spurted out all over the room. Some of it even landed on my mom."

Blake stopped for a moment to catch his breath.

"Finally," he continued, "our father passed out from the pain, and the men got tired of beating him. One of the guys looked right into my eyes and smiled while saying, *"Take this as a life lesson kid. If you let a woman screw you, this is how you'll end up."* Then he put his gun against my father's temple and pulled the trigger. My mother screamed as my dad's brains splattered over the side of her face."

"Oh my gosh, Blake," Jewell whispered, and tears were now running down her face.

Blake had to look away from her. He'd never be able finish his story if he focused on the sympathy in her eyes. And he needed to finish.

"My mother actually thanked the man, and then begged for her life. He laughed at her while he ran the gun up and down her face. He told her that if she pleased him real well, he'd let her live. The next hour was almost worse than any other part of the evening, because that's exactly what she did, even as the sickening smell our father's blood was filling up the room. We closed our eyes, but we heard everything. The two men beat the hell out of my mother while doing unimaginable things to her at the same time. At one point I opened my eyes because she told them to go ahead and kill us too, that we would inform on them if they didn't. She looked at me as she said it. Blood was dripping from her mouth, and all I saw was hatred in her eyes…" Blake was shocked when he found a strange tightness in his throat. Why should this upset him? He hated his mother and even his father. This story shouldn't affect him in the least.

"Blake, oh, Blake, I am so sorry," Jewell said as she rose

from her chair. Before he could stop her, she sat down in his lap and wrapped her arms around him.

The tightness in his throat grew even harder to fight, but fight it he did. He needed to keep talking, to get this over with. It was several moments before he could continue, and when he did, his voice was flat. He refused to let emotion overwhelm him.

"When the men grew bored, the shot my mother in the head and left her lying on the floor, then threw my father over her. I'll never forget the sight of my parents' blood seeping from their bodies. To this day I will never own red carpet."

Jewell wasn't impressed by Blake's attempt at a joke.

"Don't do that, Blake. Don't try to make light of this to show how strong you are. I know you're strong, I get it, but there are some things no one is strong enough to deal with."

"My mother had given the staff the day off, of course, because she didn't want adult witnesses, so my brothers and I spent the whole night tied up on the couch there in the room with our dead parents. When the maid came in the next day, she found us and called the cops."

"But every time you close your eyes, it's like being right back there, isn't it?" Jewell asked.

"Not every time, Jewell, not since meeting you," he said, and he felt her body tense. Had he just revealed too much to her? Blake decided to stop talking now, afraid of what was going to come from his mouth.

"That's way too much responsibility to put on my shoulders," she gasped.

"I'm just speaking the truth."

"You aren't exactly what you portray, are you, Blake?"

He didn't want to give her false illusions of who he was. Withdrawing back into himself, he pulled her head back so she'd be forced to look into his eyes.

"I'm a cold bastard, Jewell. Around you, I want to be different, but I will never really change from who I am. Take that as a warning," he said before leaning down and kissing her.

He wanted to bring heat and hunger, but he couldn't right now. So he settled for a chaste but hard kiss to remind her of who he was. Yes, he'd been through a traumatic experience, but he'd still made choices that only he could make. He owned those choices.

"I don't think you're as cold as you want the world to think you are," she countered. When he was clearly about to reply, she held up her hand to stop him. "Fine, Blake. We are both screwed up, probably too screwed up to ever discover real happiness. So what the heck? I'll marry you. I'll do what you want."

It took a few moments for her words to sink in. But Blake didn't feel the triumph that he'd expected to feel. He'd told her his story and now she felt sorry for him. That wasn't what he wanted — not at all.

"I don't need your sympathy, Jewell," he growled.

"Whether you want it or not, you have it."

"Don't think I'm going to change just for you," he told her.

"Have you changed your mind about getting married, Blake?"

That stopped him. "No, I still think we should marry," he told her. "I just don't want you to think it's going to be a traditional sort of marriage."

"I would never think that," she said, and her sad sigh

made that tightness reappear in his throat.

But Blake had just gotten what he wanted, and he wasn't going to let the guilt consuming him change the course his life was going to take. Jewell would be his wife.

CHAPTER TWENTY-TWO

"SAVE YOURSELF!"

Startled, Jewell lost her hold on her cup of coffee, and was thankful that it bounced into the sink. Timing was everything!

She couldn't help but smile when she turned around and saw Justin come running into the room with Blake hot on his trail.

"Help, Sissy," Justin hollered, but the words were scrambled because he was laughing so hard.

"There is no help for the two of you," Jewell said with mock weariness, and then began laughing when Justin's socks made him go skidding across the well-polished tile floors.

The boy landed in a heap near her feet. Thanks to the counter, Blake barely managed to come to a stop; he might have landed with a splat right on top of Justin.

The last three weeks had passed in a blur for her. When Blake said he could get things done, he hadn't been fooling around. They'd gotten a court date within two weeks — for mere mortals, that would have been miraculous — and been granted temporary custody of Justin, and the three of them had been living in Blake's new home since they had brought the boy home a week ago.

So quickly that it made her head spin, they had gotten into a routine. They got up together and had breakfast, and then Justin went to school while Blake and Jewell headed off to work. She loved her new job with Dr. Rice. It gave her purpose and she felt, for the first time in a long while, as if she was in control.

Maybe not complete control, as she was very unsure of where she and Blake stood, but at least there was some stability in her life, and most importantly, she had Justin back. She would do nothing to screw that up.

One thing about the situation baffled her. Blake hadn't touched her since they'd moved in together. She didn't even share a room with him. Since she'd agreed to the marriage of convenience, she hadn't heard him utter another word about it.

And her fear that this was all a dream prevented her from bringing it up again, though she thought about it almost constantly. How could she not when she was around him so much?

Blake was standing there in a low-slung pair of sweats and a tight T-shirt, his normal morning attire. When he reached up for a mug and then poured himself some coffee, she couldn't help but appreciate his incredible physique.

She also couldn't help but wonder whether he now thought this hadn't been such a great idea. Still, he was amazing with Justin. Maybe he really had just needed someone to make the business deal go through, and in the meantime he was getting attached to her little brother.

Jewell didn't know what to think anymore. Elsa worked part time for them, cleaning and cooking on occasion, but other than that, she and Blake split the household responsibilities.

They seemed to be nothing more than housemates.

"What are your plans tonight?" he asked as he got out the cereal for Justin while the boy reached into the cupboard for a bowl.

"The girls at work asked if I wanted to go out for a drink tonight," she told him. "I'm pretty excited about it, actually. It's been a really long time since I've been asked to go anywhere with someone."

"Ah, that's good," he replied, but the expression on his face didn't match his words.

"Is there something wrong?" she asked as she racked her brain for something she might have missed. "Is something going on later today that I've forgotten about?"

"Not at all," he replied, but he'd lost all the joy he'd displayed when he and Justin had first hurtled into the kitchen.

A sense of guilt followed her around while she changed for work and said her goodbyes, but she didn't understand what she could possibly be feeling guilty about. She hadn't done anything wrong, had she?

Blake surprised her when he met her at the front door, his eyes unreadable. "Have a nice day at work," he told her, and he kissed her on the cheek.

She walked to her new car and climbed in almost in a daze. If only she could read him. After all, she was living with the guy. But it seemed that nothing would come easy between two of them.

Jewell made it to work early and sat in her car for a moment to look at the building the doctor's office was in. She felt pride when she walked through the beautiful front doors and said hello to the receptionist before heading to the back rooms, where her office was.

No, her job wasn't exciting, but she'd had enough excitement in the last year to last her a lifetime. What she absolutely craved right now was peace, normalcy, and the absence of any further disasters in her life.

Did she miss the passion she'd shared with Blake? Well, sure she did, but she'd lived all but four months of her life without having it or missing it, so she could certainly get used to living without it again.

She might even have a chance to find true love one day — romance and passion both. It wasn't as if she were an old maid, to use a ridiculously dated and sexist term. Yes, she'd have Justin at home with her for the next ten years, but a lot of people had patchwork families, and having a child didn't scare every guy off.

If only the thought of being with another man was in the least appealing.

Her day flew past, and when five o'clock arrived, Jewell was more than ready for some girl time.

"Jewell, let's get the heck out of here. It's Friday night and I'm hoping to find some cold drinks and some hot men."

Jewell looked up at her co-worker, Stacy, a single mom in her late twenties who maybe partied a bit too much, but who was said to be a fun person to hit the town with.

"Who's coming?" Jewell asked after she shut down her computer and was putting on her coat.

"A couple of the nurses and the new receptionist. I hope

you plan on staying out late," Stacy remarked as the two of them made their way to the elevator.

"Are we meeting there?" Jewell asked her.

"We should carpool. Jenna has agreed to be the designated driver tonight," Stacy said, and she grabbed Jewell's hand and led her to a minivan in the corner of the lot. Four other women were standing there.

"I have had a crap week. Let's get there before all the tables are gone," Jenna said. She unlocked the van and the women piled in.

It didn't take them long to get to the bar, and within an hour Jewell was more than ready to go home. This just wasn't her scene, and she would much rather have been spending time with Justin — okay, and with Blake, if she were forced to admit it — than with a bunch of women intent on getting drunk.

"May I have this dance?"

Jewell looked up at a nicely dressed man who was gazing down at her as if she were his next meal. The refusal was on her tongue when Stacy leaned over and whispered in her ear. "Yum…he's beyond hot. Go for it."

Jewell found herself being pushed from her seat and led to the dance floor. Maybe it was the two drinks she'd consumed, and maybe it was depression from feeling unwanted by the man she so wanted to want her, but one dance turned into two and then three, and soon she found herself sitting at a corner table with Frank. The guy was telling her the story of his freaking life! Sheesh!

The only thing keeping her sitting there was the hope that maybe by receiving a little bit of male attention she could somehow push away her all-consuming feelings for Blake.

So far, that wasn't happening.

CHAPTER TWENTY-THREE

AN HOUR LATER, Jewell was waiting for a break in the conversation, an acceptable opportunity for her to excuse herself. She wasn't in any way attracted to Frank, who obviously thought work was his life, and she was hoping to make it home in time to watch a movie with Justin and Blake That was far more her idea of a perfect Friday night than sitting here with a man who was starting to drop heavy hints the way he wanted the evening to progress.

"I've enjoyed spending time with you tonight," Frank said as he reached across the table and took her hand before she could pull it away. "I'd like to continue this somewhere…quieter."

He ran across her knuckles, and she shuddered.

The guy wasn't taking the normal social cues she was giving him, cues that should have told him she just wasn't interested in what he had to offer. But before she was able to respond to his suggestion, he continued.

"We're both attractive people with needs and the two of

us have a connection," he said with what she was assuming he thought was a seductive grin.

This had to stop now.

"Frank, I really appreciate the dancing tonight, and the drink you bought me, and company, but I'm not interested in starting a relationship. I just wanted to come out with my girlfriends for a few hours. I'm sure I'm not the only woman in here who is looking for something that might last longer than an hour," she said with a gentle smile.

No one wanted to be rejected and she wasn't out to mislead this man or hurt his pride.

"Oh, I wasn't expecting that. It seemed like we've had something going on tonight," he said, still holding her fingers. "Is there any possibility that you might change your mind?"

"No. I've had a rough year, really, and I'm just not on the market, so to speak. Sorry, Frank."

He looked disappointed but certainly not devastated, which made her feel better. Of course, why would he be too upset? It wasn't as if they knew each other, not after an hour in a club.

She looked away from him at all the people, at the men leaning against the bar and flirting with women, at the groups sitting around tables and engaging in serious people-watching, and she could almost guess which people were hoping to hook up with someone and those who just wanted a little down time after a long workweek.

She wasn't really in either category. She'd just wanted to do some female bonding, but it seemed that she wasn't at all tuned in to everyone else's idea of night life. She'd worked too hard during college and afterward, and though she was only in her twenty-four, she felt so much older.

Maybe taking on the responsibility of caring for her mother before she died and of raising her little brother had aged her. She really didn't know.

"Well, I'm just out celebrating tonight anyway, Jewell. I wasn't really looking to hook up with someone, but then I saw you and couldn't seem to take my eyes off you, so I thought *what the heck*. But I get it. I was in a relationship last year that threw me for a loop when it ended. I haven't gotten serious with anyone since."

"I'm sorry about that. Maybe a bar isn't the best place to go hunting for a nice girl," she said with a friendly smile.

"Yeah, you're probably right about that," he said with a small chuckle.

"I'm really ready to go home," she told him. She was finished with this for the night.

"Let me walk you out," he said as he stood and held out a hand.

She gave him her hand and stood up, then allowed him to escort her back to the table where her co-workers — other than poor Jenna — were feeling a buzz from the large quantities of alcohol they'd been consuming. They barely registered her telling them she was going to call a cab and head home.

"Good friends?" Frank asked, making Jewell laugh.

"New co-workers," she informed him.

The valet called a cab and Frank waited with her in the chilly evening air. When the cab arrived, she turned to thank him and he pulled her to him for a hug. "Thank you for a wonderful evening. I hope to run into you again," he said, and she could see he was hoping to get her phone number.

"I don't think that will happen, but it was a pleasure

talking with you tonight," she told him gently. She quickly hugged him back and then pulled away when it went a bit too long.

"I can always hope," he said as he held open the cab door.

Jewell didn't bother replying this time. She wasn't giving him her number, and she didn't want him to hold out on any hope that she'd see him again. This was her last time for a ladies' night out. She'd tried it and it had failed.

Jewell hoped Blake didn't notice it when she returned home in a cab. Though she'd have to ask him for a ride to her car tomorrow, she just hoped to make it home tonight while Justin was still awake.

When they pulled up to the house, though, the lights were off in the living room, and her hope was dashed. It was only ten in the evening, but a lot had happened this week for Justin, too, with a new school, a new home, and moving in with a man he certainly liked and respected, but didn't know all that well.

Her brother was a real trouper to have such positive attitude after so much change had been thrown at him.

She paid the cab driver, then made her way up the path to the front door and fumbled in her purse for what had to be a full minute before she found her keys and let herself inside.

All of a sudden, loneliness like she hadn't experienced in a while weighed down on her, and she fought the urge to run to Blake's room and demand he give her some TLC. But that, she knew, would only ease the loneliness for a short time. She needed a long-term solution.

If she hadn't been so afraid of rocking the boat she was riding in, she might have opened up and told him she was feeling this way. But what if he was somehow disgusted with that and got rid of her? Justin's life would be thrown into upheaval again. No. It was better to just go with the flow, even if she felt like she was constantly fighting the current.

Jewell set down her purse, and then smiled when she heard a squeak. The kitten they'd gotten the day after Justin had come to live with them was winding its tiny orange body around her feet.

"At least someone has missed me," she whispered. She lifted up the little boy fur and nuzzled his soft fur, delighting in the purrs he released amid its high-pitched mews of satisfaction at being held.

When she stepped into the living room and found Blake sitting back with only a dim lamp lit and an unreadable expression on his face, she stopped. "Why are you sitting here like this?" she asked, looking around.

When Blake was at home, he was almost always working, either in his office or in his favorite chair in the living room, and one thing she knew about him was that he really liked lots of light. She was always turning it off in the rooms he exited, and he often laughed at her about her compulsiveness.

When she moved again, she noticed a bottle of bourbon on the table beside him, and an empty crystal glass next to it. That didn't look good.

As she drew nearer, she noticed his muscles were tense, and the look in his eyes wasn't as casual as she'd first thought. No, his eyes were burning. She'd seen that look before, not that she was able to interpret it.

"Is everything okay, Blake? Is Justin okay?" she asked, getting ready to bolt for the stairs to assure herself that

Justin was still there, that he was fine.

"Justin went to sleep two hours ago. It's been a busy week for him," Blake said, and her heartbeat slowed just the tiniest bit until he stood up and began moving toward her.

Jewell didn't know why she took a step backward, but there was something dangerous in his eyes, and every muscle in her body was screaming at her to run. She knew that was foolish, but at the same time, her instincts were most likely right.

"Put down the kitten, Jewell," he told her as he drew ever closer.

Jewell had almost forgotten about the kitten. "Oh," she said as she freed the little fur ball and watched as he ran off, probably to destroy something.

"You're really worrying me, Blake. What in the world is the matter?" she asked as she took another involuntary step backward.

"I have given you time to adjust, have waited for you to tell me you're ready, have moved in together with you, reunited you and your brother, and still I've waited, and I haven't gotten the green light from you," he said, and she stepped back yet again.

"What in the world are you talking about, Blake?"

"Since rescuing you from Relinquish Control, I've only had you two nights. And it's been over three weeks since the last time we were together — *three weeks*, Jewell. And then tonight you go out with another man," he said, his muscles flexing, his eyes sparking.

"What? I didn't go out with another man," she told him, though she didn't understand why she was denying it. "That wouldn't be your business anyway," she said, suddenly tired of being defensive when she didn't even know why she was being that way.

"Max was there," he told her.

"I didn't see him," she began before stopping. "Then why in the world didn't he give me a ride home?"

"I wanted him there to make sure you were safe. Apparently you were more than safe," Blake said, his voice menacingly low.

"I don't need someone to spy on me, Blake," she told him. She didn't get to say anything more, though.

Blake must have decided they had conversed enough, because one second they were facing off against each other and the next second she was completely out of breath. He'd reached out and grabbed her, hauling her body against his before lifting her in the air.

And then they were moving — right toward his bedroom.

CHAPTER TWENTY-FOUR

BLAKE PUSHED HIS bedroom door open with his foot, and shut it the same way. Jewell was so shocked by his behavior that she uttered not a word of protest. And then she was airborne for a brief moment before the bed caught her.

She was trying to clear her head, but his scent enveloped her, and all she could do was to inhale the musk of the only man she had ever desired.

Still, he was behaving like a brute, and she thought about trying to stop him — for about two seconds — but then he was on the bed with her, his legs pinning hers down as he pulled off her coat, shirt and bra in a quick sweep, leaving her upper half bare to his view. He moved to the side, but only to yank off her pants and minuscule panties, and now he was ripping his own clothes from his body.

It was so fast — all of it was happening far too fast.

Before she was able to protest, Blake was stretching his now naked body on top of her, and the feel of his solid chest pressing against her tender breasts made her cry out his name in pleasure.

"Yes, Jewell," he told her, "the only name you'll ever say like that is mine." His lips captured hers, subduing her moans of pleasure.

His mouth trailed down the side of her throat, where she knew he'd feel the pounding of her pulse, but she didn't care. He made her burn, and as much as she hated the weakness, she felt too damn good at the moment to have any regrets.

"I can't believe I kept from touching you so long," he said, and he circled her nipples with his lips and nipped the tender peaks before washing them, soothing them with his tongue.

He slowly moved his mouth up between her breasts and then he was kissing her again, invading her mouth with his tongue while his solid erection pressed against her core. She couldn't help but spread her legs out wider as her body begged his to make her complete.

"Please, Blake, please fill me," she groaned. She planted her feet on the bed and lifted her hips, urging him to join with her.

It had been too long since they'd last made love, and she wanted fulfillment, she wanted the two of them to be as one, and she wanted it right now. Her passion was overwhelming in its intensity.

Blake didn't answer her plea; he instead gripped her hair and angled her head just the way he wanted it, the better to devour her mouth, while he rubbed his hardness on the outside of her wet core, letting it help lubricate him, prepare him for entry.

"Now, Blake, please," she said again as she pushed up

against him.

She raked her fingernails down his back and gripped his muscular behind in her desperation to have him inside her. If he wanted her to beg, then she would beg, but she would also take all of him she could take.

"How much do you want me, Jewell?" he asked as he reached for her hands, took both arms, and, holding her wrists with one hand, pushed her arms above her head.

"I want you, Blake. I need you. I need you now," she practically sobbed. To hell with power games. She wasn't in the mood for anything but completion.

He rewarded her for those words by reaching down between them and slipping his fingers inside her hot core while stroking her aching bundle of nerves with his thumb. She cried out when only a few flicks of his masterful fingers brought her release, her body tightening, her heart thundering.

"Yes," he sighed. "You are so responsive, my Jewell." And before she could even think about catching her breath, he pulled his fingers from her and moved them upward to cup her breast and squeeze her nipple at the same time as he thrust hard inside her, nearly bringing her to orgasm again right then.

Time lost meaning, and something seemed to come over Blake. She felt his thrusts, each and every one of them, as he moved his hips, pushing in and pulling out of her. Moans tumbled from her throat while he growled words of praise and pleasure almost in time to their frantic lovemaking.

Sweat slickened their bodies as the inferno built higher and higher and each time Blake ravaged her mouth along with her body, she felt almost as if she were floating above herself, watching this exquisite moment while still feeling each and everything he did to her.

Jewell knew she was forever lost to this man, because no matter how long they were apart, the instant she was in his arms again, she belonged to him, only him, and it was right where she needed and wanted to be.

"Come for me, Jewell. Squeeze me tight," he commanded her.

She gave him exactly what he wanted and demanded. Her body let go and she cried out his name over and over again as her body convulsed around him and she felt the release in every cell, every atom. He continued pumping inside her, drawing the orgasm out, making her pulse over and over again until she didn't think she could bear it any longer.

She felt as if she were gliding along in the sky, and during that moment, that moment where the release began to ebb, she heard him cry out as he tensed, buried deep inside her, and then he shook, his own release washed through him, his hardness sending his seed deep into her womb.

Blake collapsed against her, and their bodies were both burning up. She clung tightly to him, not willing to let this moment go, not willing to free him from her hold. She was exactly where she wanted to be and fear, fear that the moment would end the second they spoke, kept her cleaving desperately to his embrace.

But soon the moment faded, and Jewell felt almost bereft when Blake rolled off her. Her limbs grew cold, and an ache and an emptiness unlike anything she'd known before was filling her stomach.

"You belong to me, Jewell. I won't share you with other

men," Blake told her. He reached for her again, pulling her tightly against his side.

"What are you talking about, Blake?"

"The man at the bar. You shouldn't have done that."

"The man at the bar?" She was lost for a few moments in her sex-induced coma. Then her eyes snapped open, and Jewell drew back so she could look at Blake. "Wait! Was that was this was about? Another man spoke to me, so you had to fuck me to show me you're better?" she asked with horror.

"No," he said, his voice almost deadly. "I have been holding back because I thought that was what you wanted — needed. When you allowed yourself to be vulnerable with another man, I decided it was time for me to remind you I was here," he told her, not releasing his hold on her. "Ready, and definitely waiting."

"But...this makes no sense, Blake. We've seen each other almost daily for weeks and you haven't touched me, and then we've lived in this house just over a week and still you haven't touched me. Why would my speaking to another man upset you?"

"I told you, I was trying to give you space. But I'm done with that now. I'm so hungry for you, I can't even think straight. And you are just as hungry for me. I could hardly miss your response to me just now. We belong together and it's time you just accept that."

He rolled back on top of her and pressed against her core. She wasn't even surprised when her body instantly responded to his.

"I just assumed you knew you had made a mistake, Blake, that you knew it couldn't possibly work between us," she told him. Why not? While lying in his arms fully naked, she couldn't hide any of her body's secrets from him. She might as well open her heart up too. If he was going to crush her, she'd rather he do it in one fell swoop than keep dragging her suffering out relentlessly.

"You assumed wrong, Jewell. What we have here, so to speak, is a failure of communication, and that's going to end right now. I *will* marry you," he said, making her heart skip a beat before he continued. "I'll do it for the business deal and for your brother and because this thirst you make me feel will never be quenched."

His words hurt her more than she would ever admit to him, but she was also powerless to fight him anymore. She'd already agreed to marry this man, and her future was in his hands. One thing that she had confidence in was that, at least for a while, the two of them would be able to please each other well. The fire that burned so hot didn't appear to be running out of fuel.

Jewell covered up her sadness by reaching for his head and pulling him down to her, by being the one to initiate the kiss this time. When he groaned into her mouth, she felt her sense of emptiness begin to ease. Yes, their relationship was nowhere near perfect or conventional, but it was working, and Jewell knew she was already in too deep to make it out unscathed if he should leave her. So she really had nothing to lose by giving herself to him completely.

"I want you, Blake," she said, instead of saying what she so desperately wanted to say.

Blake didn't reply. His body joined with hers, and he loved her again until the early hours of the morning.

CHAPTER TWENTY-FIVE

TYLER AND BYRON looked at Blake and Jewell with varying expressions on their faces. Jewell shifted nervously on her feet, looked up at Byron's black eyes, and then down at the floor. She had always thought Blake was intimidating. Well, Blake seemed to have nothing on this little brother. Byron was terrifying.

When she next looked up, she found Tyler beaming at her, and then before she could even think of stopping him, he rushed over, took her from Blake's arms, and wrapped her in his. "Congratulations, Jewell. I'm delighted to welcome you to our family," he said. He then bent down and gave her a loud, smacking kiss.

"Okay, that's enough," Blake grumbled as he pulled her away from his overly enthusiastic brother.

"Aw, come on, Blake. She isn't married yet," Tyler said with a laugh, and Jewell had to cover her own smile when she saw Blake's eye twitch. She rubbed his arm, and he turned his look from his brother to her, and then she watched a miracle happen — his shoulders relaxed and the sparkle returned to his eyes.

"Sorry, Jewell, I know Tyler is doing it to get a reaction from me, but when I even think of another man touching you, it fills me with rage, so think how I feel when I have to stand here and witness it." With a rueful smile, he brushed his lips lightly against hers.

"I am going to tell you a secret," she said quietly, and he leaned closer. "I love that you are possessive. Just don't be ridiculously so," she added, and gave him a kiss. There was protective and then there was psycho. She didn't want Blake to cross over the line into boiling bunnies on her kitchen stove.

"I knew it was going to happen anyway. Blake has been a mess since meeting you," Tyler said.

Blake stiffened. "I am not a mess, Tyler," he said indignantly.

"Sure, brother," Tyler told him. "It's okay; really it is. Even the hardest of asses fall eventually."

"I don't see that it's funny to mock a man who's under the thumb of a woman," Byron said. Then he turned his eyes on Jewell and she felt singed to the spot.

"Back off, Byron," Blake warned his brother. "This isn't about you."

"It sure as hell is about me. Anything to do with our family is about all of us," Byron said. Jewell watched as both brothers' shoulders stiffened, and she grew scared as sin as they tried to stare each other down.

"Oh, come on, guys. This is a special occasion," Tyler said, and Jewell noticed how he moved just slightly so he was standing between his two brothers.

Was fighting a normal thing between them? And did Tyler often break it up? She was too afraid to even speak as the tension continued to mount despite Tyler's attempt at intervention.

"And when is the happy day?" Byron practically sneered.

Jewell wished she weren't standing there now, because the fireworks were just about to really start. But Blake's arm was wrapped around her, and she really had no choice but to witness the explosions when Blake answered Byron's question.

"Tomorrow," Blake said.

"Tomorrow?" Byron practically thundered.

"Do you have a problem with my wedding date?" Blake asked tautly.

"Why in the hell are you rushing this?"

"I don't see why that's any of your business."

"It's my business," Byron told him, "because I don't understand why you're allowing yourself to be snatched up by some woman who is obviously out to get whatever she can from you."

Jewell's mouth dropped when Blake released her so fast she nearly tripped, and then she was watching his fist come up and knock Byron in the side of the jaw. She had no idea what to do. There was no doubt in her mind that Byron would retaliate. Men and their machismo…

Instead, after turning his head and spitting out a bit of blood, the man looked straight at his brother, who was staring daggers at him. "I'll let that one pass, Blake, since you're obviously screwed up in the head right now," Byron said.

"Who in the hell do you think you are?" Blake shouted.

"I'm the brother who has been with you through thick and thin, and I'm the one you normally would listen to.

Don't you realize this woman has you so messed up that you're choosing to please her even if it upsets the balance of your family?"

"Look, guys, emotions are high right now, but we really don't want to say something that can't be taken back later," Tyler interjected.

"I don't regret anything I'm saying," Bryon said.

"No, because you're a complete asshole, Byron. Jewell will become my wife tomorrow, and I'd like to have you there, but if you can't be, then I understand that." Blake took a step back.

Jewell was finally able to gulp in a breath of air. It looked like the fight might be over.

"I'll be there, Blake, not because I support this marriage, but because you're going to need me when you realize what a mistake you've made," Byron said, and then he looking back at Jewell and piercing her with his brutal gaze.

"I'm sorry you're so bitter," Jewell told him. "But you're wrong, Byron. I don't want to take anything from your brother." It was a moment before she even realized she'd spoken.

"Ha. A woman always has a plan," Byron replied, dismissing her words as easily as he was dismissing her.

"I won't have you there if you can't treat Jewell with respect," Blake warned his brother.

"I won't say another word to her," Byron said. "No problem."

He might not be saying another word to her, but she could feel his animosity; the very air around them all was thick with it. Jewell suspected that she and Byron would never be friends, not because she thought he was evil —

though he showed signs of being pretty dang close — but because Byron didn't seem to allow anyone to ever get close to him. It made her feel sad for him. What a lonely, thankless life the man must lead.

"Well, we got that all out of the way, so why don't we go celebrate with a nice dinner?" Tyler said a little too eagerly.

"That sounds good, Tyler," Blake told him.

Jewell was more than happy when they all left the office building, which was where Blake had decided to inform his brothers about tomorrow's wedding. It wasn't going to be a fancy wedding. It wasn't about love, after all. But still, he had managed to arrange a simple ceremony at their house. Well, at his house. Jewell didn't know whether she'd ever be able to consider it fully hers.

Yes, for the past two weeks the two of them had been getting along great. Blake had gone from demanding and arrogant to more considerate and asking her opinion. Well, everywhere except for the bedroom. There, he was insatiable and very, very demanding. And she loved it.

His business deal had to be going well, because he was happier than she'd ever seen him be. She just wished he were happy for a different reason. But no, they didn't speak of love, and no, she wasn't under the illusion that they were marrying because of love. And that really sucked because somehow in the midst of all of this she was falling in love with him.

She couldn't pinpoint the moment when it had begun happening. Maybe it was like those survivor stories where two people under extreme circumstances fall in love with each other. *The Stockholm syndrome, perhaps?* she thought will a grim chuckle. Maybe it was just because she felt so dependent on him. Whatever the reasons, she was simultaneously excited about her marriage to him and dreading it.

This was a fairy tale, Jewell knew, but a fractured one. She wasn't a princess, and Blake most certainly was not Prince Charming. This long, strange dream seemed almost certain to end in a rude awakening.

Byron backed down a little during the dinner they shared that evening, and later that night the brothers took Blake with them for an impromptu bachelor party. Jewell was restless, tossing and turning for hours in her lonely bed.

Wasn't the night before a woman's wedding day supposed to be filled with dreams of happily-ever-afters? Not for her. Hadn't she decided long ago that she wasn't one of those people who was destined to win that perfect life? Still, she was luckier than most, she reminded herself.

She had her brother and she had Blake — for now.

CHAPTER TWENTY-SIX

"YOU DO REALIZE that if you don't breathe, you're going to pass out, don't you?"

Jewell met McKenzie's gaze in the mirror and she attempted a smile, but there was no power great enough to accomplish that. Her stomach was nervous, her eyes almost wild, and her body felt as if it didn't even belong to her.

"What if I'm making the biggest mistake of my life?" Jewell asked.

McKenzie knelt down by her and turned her chair. "Jewell, I've made many mistakes in my lifetime, so trust me when I tell you, this isn't a mistake," she said, and she completely surprised Jewell when she leaned in and gave her a hug.

McKenzie looked so much softer in her light blue chiffon dress, which brushed the top of her knees in the front and flowed down in the back. Her makeup was minimal — she possessed an amazing natural beauty — and her hair was up in a stylish bun with a few strands falling around her face in a lovely frame.

It was odd, but she looked so different, so...*innocent* was the word that kept popping into Jewell's mind, that it calmed the jittery bride. "You've been good to me these last few months, McKenzie. I don't know how I can ever repay you," Jewell said, feeling tears trying to break through.

"I like you, Jewell. I didn't expect to find friendship with you, but I genuinely like you," McKenzie told her.

"I like you, too, McKenzie," Jewell said. "And maybe someday you will tell me your story. You know mine, after all."

"I might just do that," McKenzie replied, instead of retreating into silence the way Jewell expected her to do. "But right now it is your wedding day, and you have an anxious groom out there waiting on you."

"I don't think he's anxious, McKenzie. Remember, this is for his business deal," Jewell said with more sadness than she cared to admit she was feeling. "And, of course, so I can get Justin back permanently."

"You can say anything you want to make yourself feel better, but I know that look in a woman's eyes. You love him, Jewell."

"I...I'm doing this for Justin," Jewell insisted, though the words got trapped in her throat.

"You've done a lot for your brother," McKenzie said, and then a look in her eyes alerted Jewell to the depths of pain this woman had borne for some reason. "Just remember to not lose yourself," she added. "Enough of this, though. Let's focus on what matters today — your wedding."

"If you need to talk, I'm always here to listen," Jewell

told her.

"I think I know that," McKenzie said with a shaky smile. "Now sit down. Let's get this veil on you and get you down that aisle. I think the groom will start manhandling people if you don't get out there on time."

If only that were true, Jewell thought. But no, this was a business deal. If she was developing feelings for Blake, they were unimportant. This wasn't about her, or about Blake for that matter. It was about her little brother and doing everything she could for him.

And it was absurd to be so selfish, if only in her thoughts. She was getting a second chance at life, and if she dared to ask for too much, then she was setting herself up for heartbreak. She had Justin, she had an incredible sex life with Blake, and she had security. That was more than so many people had, so she would damn well smile and appreciate her blessings instead of focusing on what she lacked.

Her veil in place, Jewell turned to look at the image of herself in he mirror. Her gown was simple, made of white chiffon that flowed to the ground, with delicate beadwork on the bodice, and with sleeves that billowed until they reached her wrists. The dress was molded to her torso, and it floated around her legs, making her feel like she was walking through a breeze with each step she took.

Even her jewel-encrusted shoes sparkled as her toes peeked out with each step she took. She looked like a happy bride, and she was surprised by how quickly the wedding had come together. She'd expected nothing more than a quick exchange of vows in front of the justice of the peace down at the county courthouse. So silly of her to think that a simple wedding would mean the same thing to a billionaire as it did to mere mortals like her.

They were about to wed in the backyard of their home, and every time she sat out on the deck, she'd be able to remember this day. And when the marriage ended, as it inevitably would, she would leave this place behind and, if she was lucky, leave the memories behind too.

"You look stunning," McKenzie said as she came and stood beside her. "Blake is a very lucky man."

"Sissy, are you ready?"

They both turned to see Justin standing in the doorway. He was so grown up at only ten, looking more handsome than ever in his little black tux, his hair combed into place, and no smudges on his cheeks.

"Oh, Justin, you look wonderful," Jewell said as she bent down and held out her arms.

He didn't hesitate to run to her and wrap himself around her. "I love you so much," she told him, squeezing just a little too tight and not even thinking about her dress.

"I love you too, Sissy," he responded before he backed away and coughed as he pulled himself together.

She stood up and took her brother's hand, and they followed McKenzie out to the back doors of the house, where she heard the music begin.

"I'm so glad you're walking with me, because from here on out everything we do will be together," Jewell told Justin.

"I really love Blake, Sissy," he said, his eyes shining up at her.

"I know you do, Bubby. He loves you too," she assured him.

And then they stopped talking as the two of them proceeded through the doors and began the short walk down the red-carpeted path to the stage Blake had had set up for the occasion. When Jewell looked up, her gaze met Blake's and she stopped for a moment, her heart racing at the expression in his eyes.

For just this moment, she let go of all her worries, of all the pain she had been through, and she let go of her doubts. She imagined this was all real, that she was walking down the aisle toward a man who couldn't live without her. Her lips lifted and then her smile grew when she saw the possessiveness in his eyes. That was all for her. For this moment, it was just the two of them, and everyone else simply faded away.

Bright red and orange splashed across the sky as the sun sank low over the horizon, and with the music playing, no scene could have been set more perfectly. Only a few people were there to witness this marriage, and it was just the way she wanted it.

Standing next to Blake was Tyler, and, surprisingly, Byron was with him. Though Byron didn't support this marriage, he did support his brother, and that showed Jewell that the man wasn't as hard as he wanted everyone to think he was. There was hope for him yet.

Finally, she arrived at the altar, and Justin took his role very seriously as he handed her over to Blake and then went to stand beside him, beside the man who would raise him — at least for as long as Blake wanted to stay a part of their lives. Jewell had only McKenzie next to her, and that was just fine. The woman had become her friend, and as it was because of McKenzie that Jewell had met Blake, it seemed quite fitting to have her standing there with them.

If anyone had asked Jewell what was said during the exchange of vows, she wouldn't have been able to answer.

But she gazed into Blake's eyes so long and so intently that she certainly would have been able to describe the look on his face and the way his hand felt clasped in hers.

Yes, McKenzie was right. She was in love with this man, a man she never should have fallen in love with. And she didn't care. A person could choose the people they acquainted themselves with, but they couldn't choose the one their heart decided to let in.

"I now pronounce you man and wife. You may kiss the bride."

The air was swept from Jewell's lungs as Blake pulled her into his arms and took her mouth in a kiss that sealed them together as one. She melted against him and felt almost in a daze when he pulled back and she looked up at the sparkle in his eyes.

"Now you are forever mine, Jewell," he whispered for only her to hear.

"I think I have been from the day we met," she replied, making his lips turn up.

"We're a family now," Blake told her, and he held out his free arm to Justin, who eagerly stepped up to them and threw his arms around his new uncle.

"Yes, we are," Jewell said as tears flowed down her face.

As the three of them walked back down the aisle, Jewell's heart was filled with joy. Her only hope right then was that this joy would last.

CHAPTER TWENTY-SEVEN

"HOW LONG CAN it possibly take someone to change?" Blake growled. He slammed down a shot of bourbon and glared at his brother.

Tyler laughed and Byron scoffed as they stood at the bar and gazed out at the lights hanging from the trees.

"You know women, Blake. They have to be perfect," Tyler said.

Byron downed his own shot. "Or they like to play games and see how antsy they can make you," Byron added as he sent a glare toward McKenzie, who was currently dancing with Justin.

"You seem to be staring at Ms. Beaumont quiet a bit," Tyler said, and punched Byron in the arm.

"What in the hell are you talking about?" Byron thundered.

"I'm just calling it as I see it," Tyler said with a wink and a shrug.

"I've been a mess today, and even I've noticed it," Blake said with the first smile he'd displayed since Jewell had left.

"You can both go to hell. I think I'm going to have a talk with Ms. Beaumont," Byron said, and he stormed off.

"Should we protect her?" Tyler asked as he watched McKenzie tense when Byron walked up to her.

"Hell, I think we should protect Byron," Blake replied. "McKenzie is one tough woman."

The temporary distraction had helped, but as soon as the conversation died back down, Blake was eager and anxious to see his new bride. She had looked beyond beautiful in her wedding gown, and as she'd walked toward him earlier, it had taken all his finely honed willpower to remain standing on the stage while he waited for her. He'd been sorely tempted to rush to her side and sweep her into his arms, and his heart hadn't slowed its beat until she'd said her vows and he'd sealed those vows with a kiss.

"You may be right," Tyler said with a chuckle as they watched McKenzie shove Byron away and then storm away. "Quite impressive she can stomp off with such elegance, and while wearing those stilt-like heels."

"I'm done here," Blake said.

"What?" Tyler blinked in confusion.

"I want my bride." And that was the end of the conversation. Blake walked away from Tyler, knowing his brothers would lock the place up as they left. Justin was going with McKenzie for the night, and everything else was taken care of. It was time for him to seal Jewell to him for the rest of their lives. Once they made love, the wedding was officially complete.

There was something about this woman that made him feel like a caged animal. He had spent the better part of his years on earth as a shell of a man, not feeling the colors of life, but living in black and white instead. Jewell made him feel things and do things that he'd never wanted to feel or do before. And he actually liked being out of control, even being powerless because of this woman.

He took the stairs three at a time, and he paused at their bedroom door and took a deep breath. He hoped he wouldn't frighten her with his eagerness. This night was theirs together — he needed to remember that.

When he pushed the door open, his heart nearly stopped when he found Jewell lying on the bed in a silken nightgown. The sound of the door made her jump, and then their eyes met and Blake felt his heart hammering out of control again.

"You take my breath away," he gasped. He strode up to the bed and dropped to his knees, the desire to worship her overpowering him.

She sat up with her legs dangling off the bed, and she reached for him and let her fingers sift through his hair. "I was going to say the same about you," she replied softly.

Blake couldn't move for a few seconds. The urge to rip her nightie from her body and plunge right inside of her was so potent that he was afraid he might turn into a complete animal. He had to get himself under control.

They had made love frantically many times. Tonight was about a more perfect union, about binding them together, about joining them in a way that would ensure they never parted. He didn't want to ruin this moment for either of them.

Instead of shredding their clothes, he tugged on her legs to bring her to the edge of the bed and he rested his head on her bare thigh, inhaling her perfume as he gently caressed her legs with his fingers. He paused to savor this moment, and then he turned his head and kissed her leg, swirling his tongue on her smooth, sweet skin.

A shudder passed through her, and Blake had to continue almost chanting to himself: *go slow*; *remain calm*. It wasn't an easy task when such a delectable was right in front of him. "Jewell, you make me come unglued," he whispered before standing up and backing away.

Jewell whimpered when he broke contact, and that sound went straight to his gut. He gently pushed her back up the bed and crawled over her, straddling her as she lay beneath him, her chest heaving, her eyes burning.

Blake leaned down and tenderly took her lips, caressing them, tasting them, feeling their softness with his tongue and lips. "So beautiful," he murmured as he trailed his lips down her throat and took the strap on her nightgown with his teeth and pulled it down her arm.

When he removed the gown, leaving her bare before him, he leaned back to behold her body. "No matter how many times I see you like this, I am still awed," he murmured.

She reached for him, a moan escaping her beautiful lips as she pulled him back onto her, cradling his clothed body with her naked one. Time disappeared as he rolled with her on the bed, kissing her, touching her, worshipping her.

When he finally stood so he could remove his own clothes, he found that his fingers were shaking. He tried to tell himself if was because he was so incredibly turned on, but this moment was taking him to a whole new place — a place he never wanted to leave.

After shedding his clothes quickly, he rejoined her on the bed and sighed at the perfection of their bodies pressing together with no barriers. He took his time kissing every inch of her beautiful skin, and then he was poised above her, but Blake found himself stopping before he entered her glorious heat.

"Every time I look at you like this, I can't believe I'm the one who gets to lie in your arms," he whispered.

Her eyes widened and a sheen of tears appeared. "Make love to me, Blake," she said, bringing her hands up around him and pulling him closer to her.

He surrendered to her and sank between her trembling thighs, submerging himself deep inside her.

She clung tightly to him as he thrust in and out, her hands guiding him, his name a continual cry from her well-kissed lips. And Blake got lost in her arms, hoping to never be found again as he made love to her, slowly, tenderly, with a passion he knew he could never possibly come even close to feeling with any other woman.

Looking into her eyes, he moved in perfect sync with her, and when her thighs tightened around his waist, he felt her pleasure explode around him, and he followed her into the sweet abyss.

"Mine, Jewell — you are mine forever," he told her as his body rested against hers, while her hands caressed the heated skin of his back.

"I'm yours right now, Blake."

That wasn't good enough. There were no words he could say that could possibly convey how he was feeling at this moment. It was possession, and it was passion, but it was also so much more than that. He'd never been good at putting how he felt into words, so he decided to show her in every other way that she belonged to him, and he to her.

When he knew his weight was too much for her to bear much longer, he shifted their position so she was lying on top of him now, still connected, their hearts beating in rhythm with each other. As he cradled her head against his chest, he couldn't imagine a more perfect wedding night with the wife he had chosen.

They didn't sleep the entire night. They made love and spoke of the future, and Blake gave her his heart, something he had never given to anyone else. He might not have been able to say the words, but he showed her in the only way he knew how.

CHAPTER TWENTY-EIGHT

JEWELL STRETCHED OUT her arms and was surprised to find the bed cold next to her. She slowly opened her eyes and then smiled when she found a rose and a note lying on the pillow where Blake's head should have been.

> *Good morning, beautiful. I got called in to the office to deal with an emergency. I will be home in plenty of time for our date.*
>
> *Love,*
>
> *Your husband.*

They'd been man and wife for a month now. Thirty days and thirty even better nights. No matter how many times they made love, she still felt as if she could never get enough of this man who had so suddenly entered her life and changed it overnight.

He was so different from the man she had met six

months ago, but she still saw traces of the person who had bought her from Relinquish Control, especially when they in the bedroom. The man was insatiable, but since being with him, she had discovered that she was pretty insatiable too.

No matter how many times she lay in his arms, no matter how many ways they made love, each and every time was just as exciting as the last. It was the one place she knew that Blake fully let down his guard.

Yes, he was good to her, and he was even better with Justin, but there were parts of himself that he held back, pieces of his soul he refused to share. She wasn't sure if it was because he didn't trust her completely, or if it was just because he wasn't capable of loving another human being after what he had gone through with his parents.

Either way, Jewell was both blissfully happy and, at the same time, almost unbearably lonely. She was in love with Blake, in love with this hard man who had such a beautiful soft side, and the thing that frightened her most was to realize that he might never be able to return her feelings.

She tried not to think about it too much, because if she did, she feared she wouldn't be able to honor their wedding vows into eternity. And that's what she wanted more than anything else.

She desperately wanted to speak to Blake about having children, but he never mentioned whether he was at all interested in becoming be a father. Instead, when the subject of fathers and fatherhood came up somehow, a shutter would close over his eyes and he would change the topic of conversation.

He was so good with Justin, but Justin was ten, almost eleven. There were many men, and may women for that matter, who didn't want to have their own families. Love and children had never been a condition of their marriage, and for all she knew it never would be. That didn't alter her love for him.

But as hard as she tried not to let the doubts creep into her thoughts of happiness, Jewell couldn't help but worry. She wanted a family, a real family. She wanted babies she could watch grow, and she wanted his brothers to be their uncles in every sense of the word. She wanted noisy holiday dinners, and lazy summer days at the lake. She wanted a real marriage.

Did she want too much?

For a month, she'd pushed aside her worries and tried instead to focus only on the good. But now, even when lying asleep in his arms, she felt pain, her dreams filled with visions of Blake running off with someone else, abandoning her and Justin forever to start a life with a woman he could truly love.

"Good morning, Jewell."

Jewell jumped when she stepped into the kitchen and found McKenzie sitting at the table, clutching some papers in her hands, and looking forlorn. The woman waited for Jewell to pour herself a cup of coffee.

"Hi, McKenzie. I normally love to see you, but when you're wearing that expression on your face before I've had even one cup of coffee, I tend to worry," Jewell said with a brittle laugh before she sat down, gripping her cup tightly in her hands.

She didn't even ask how McKenzie had gotten into the house, but McKenzie shared anyway. "Elsa let me in an hour ago. I've been waiting for you to wake up."

"Yes, I actually love the days Elsa works," Jewell said.

"Breakfast is so much better than the normal bowl of cereal I usually go for." But why the hell were they making small talk, she wondered, when it was more than obvious that McKenzie had something important to say.

"I…I don't know how to talk to you about this, Jewell," she said, pausing and starting again as she looked down at the table. "I…crap, this is complicated."

This was a first. McKenzie had never been afraid to meet Jewell's eyes.

"You know what they say about bad news, McKenzie — it's better to just spit it all out and get it over with," Jewell told her while gulping down her coffee. From the way McKenzie was acting, Jewell had a feeling she was going to need a lot more of the stuff to get through whatever this was.

"Jewell, you know I care about you, don't you?" McKenzie began, and Jewell's stomach clenched.

"Blake wants a divorce, right?" she said, a false bravery in her tone.

"No, nothing like that." McKenzie finally looked up and met her friend's gaze.

"I'm not a fool, McKenzie. I've known all along this isn't going to last forever. And you've always been honest with me. That's not always been pleasant, but I know I can count on you to tell me the truth."

"I promise you, Jewell, that it's not that," McKenzie said again.

"Please just tell me, McKenzie. Your hemming and hawing around it is only making it worse." Jewell got a second cup of coffee for herself and refilled McKenzie's cup as well.

Maybe the nightmares she'd been having were coming

true. Maybe a person really wasn't allowed to be too happy. She'd known that Blake was holding back from her, so having McKenzie confirm her suspicions shouldn't be so devastating, but as she waited for the woman to speak, she felt like she couldn't even breathe.

No matter which way this went, she was going to suffer through some major pain.

"It's not about Blake wanting to leave you. I think that's the last thing he would ever want to do. It's just that…" McKenzie stopped and looked down at her hands again before she looked up, sympathy in her eyes.

"It's time I tell you the truth…"

CHAPTER TWENTY-NINE

AS JEWELL WALKED blindly down the street, tears streamed down her face. McKenzie had apologized profusely for not telling her sooner, and then apologized again for telling her. She'd told her that maybe it was just better not to know the truth at all. She'd told her that it didn't matter.

But it did matter.

It mattered very much.

It was something she couldn't refute. It was about her brother — her brother and Blake. More tears fell as she continued walking. Now she knew why he'd waited three months to come back to her, and now she knew why he was able to visit with Justin when she hadn't been able to.

She was her brother's flesh and blood, the one who had been there through each new step of his life. But Blake was his father.

Blake had been a grad student, arrogant and not much different than he was today. He'd decided to donate to a sperm bank. Why not? He was gorgeous, smart, wealthy.

And he'd never planned on having children, so this way maybe someone could benefit from his genes.

Jewell hadn't known her mother had become pregnant through one of those places. She'd thought...oh, how she wished her mother were alive, wished the woman could tell her the story, tell her how this had happened. What about the man she and Justin thought was their dad. Was he even Jewell's father?

She just didn't know anything anymore, and she might never have the answers because the only person she wanted to talk to right now was no longer on this earth. Pain radiated through her entire body.

With Blake being Justin's father, he was the one with all the rights. She had none. Even though he was her brother, even though she loved him more than any other person on this earth, she had no rights to him.

But Blake wasn't a stupid man. He knew the bond Jewell had with Justin. He knew that Justin wouldn't just want to throw her away. So he'd done the one thing that would ensure he earned Justin's love — he'd married Justin's sister. And he'd slowly built a relationship with the boy. It was more than clear to Jewell that her brother loved Blake.

When all was said and done, she would be the one who was disposable. Had Blake told her any truths at all? Right now, it didn't appear to be the case. She just didn't know anything anymore, except that she was lost, and she felt more alone than she'd ever felt before.

Jewell knew they had an amazing sex life, but that wasn't enough. He would eventually grow tired of her, and then she would be the one shoved out into the cold. She would lose the man she loved with all her heart, and she would lose her little brother, the only family she had left.

Despair flowed through her, and as she made her way back to the home she now shared with Blake and Justin, she had no idea what she was going to do. She had nothing.

When she'd said this to McKenzie, her only friend in this world had given her the key to her Jewell's old apartment, which Blake had allowed McKenzie to use when her house was being remodeled. She and Blake had gone into business together, and she tried telling Jewell to talk to him, that she was sure he had an explanation.

Jewell knew Blake, though, knew him well enough to know that he might be a great business partner, but he wasn't a great husband, at least for her. Maybe to someone else he would be, but he never could be all that Jewell wanted, because what she wanted was his love.

And Blake didn't love her.

When she got back to Blake's house — she no longer felt it was hers — she opened the door and looked inside. None of this was hers. She hadn't picked the home, hadn't bought the furniture, hadn't made it a home. No, she was nothing more than a guest here.

When Blake came around the corner, he had a smile on his face, but it quickly vanished when he saw her expression. Jewell decided to push back her sadness and face him. There really was no point in dragging this out, in prolonging her agony. Neither one of them needed an emotional meltdown.

"I was worried when I came home and you weren't here," he said as he wrapped his arms around her and leaned down to kiss her lips.

When she didn't respond, he drew back, worry etched on his brow. He was a fantastic actor, she thought.

She hadn't rehearsed what she was going to say, so when the words came out, she was as surprised as he was. "Why didn't you tell me?" Her voice was flat, distant, but she watched his eyes.

And in that moment, she knew their marriage was over. He knew immediately what she was talking about. The pain rushing through her was trying to escape, but she suppressed it. There was no reason to make a scene. There was no reason for them to even talk about this.

It was over.

Her brother belonged with him — legally. Though she knew that no one would love Justin more than she could, that didn't matter. She'd fought and fought the courts. They didn't care. Blake was the boy's biological father, and he could provide a better life for Justin than she could. It was very black and white, wasn't it?

She needed to escape before she fell apart.

"Jewell, we need to talk. Let's go in the living room and I'll explain," Blake said, reaching for her. But he could see that she couldn't tolerate his touch right now. At least he was giving her enough respect to allow her to back away without chasing her.

"There's nothing to say, Blake. You found out that Justin was yours — more yours than mine — and you did what anyone would do, whatever it took to have him. And you can give him so much more than I can." She almost choked on those last words, and she had to stop.

"That's not true, Jewell. Justin loves you so much. You are his world, his everything. He needs you..." He stopped when she held up her hand.

She couldn't hear this, couldn't take his lies.

If he really felt this way, he never would have kept this

from her, never would have deceived her like this, never would have gone behind her back and stolen her brother from her.

"It's over, Blake. You don't need to pretend anymore."

Jewell turned and walked back out of the house. Nothing in it was hers — nothing. She didn't know what she was going to tell Justin, didn't know how to explain any of this to him, but right now she wasn't in any way capable of telling him anything without falling apart.

Her world had once again flipped upside down.

CHAPTER THIRTY

"DAMN!" TYLER SAID, sitting back with a stunned look on his face. "How in the hell did you keep this from us?"

"I don't want to be the one to say I told you so, but…" Byron left the sentence hanging.

"I didn't tell you because…hell, I don't know why," Blake said.

He'd never sat down with his brothers before and poured out his heart. It just wasn't something they did together, but Jewell had been gone for three days, and she refused to talk to him. She'd called the house and had spoken to Justin, and her brother — his son — was none the wiser to what was going on.

Blake didn't know how to tell Justin, and he didn't know what to think of what Jewell had done. "Maybe she's relieved," he told his brothers. "She's felt so much pressure to take care of her brother, and maybe now that she knows he'll be taken care of and loved, she is throwing up her hands and she wants to be free." He'd just admitted his biggest fear.

"Probably," Byron grumbled, but even he didn't look convinced.

"I don't think so," Tyler said. "She loves you, Blake, and she loves Justin. There's no way she would walk away unless she thought she had to."

"I don't know what else to think," Blake said with a heavy sigh.

"Think deeper. What exactly did she say? How did she act? What have you done lately?" Tyler fired off those question.

"What do you want me to say?" Blake thundered. "This isn't helping me."

"There has to be more to this than finding out you're Justin's father, though that is a big deal. But I've seen the way Jewell looks at you, and looks at her brother. She loves you both immeasurably. For her to walk away, there has to be something else going on," Tyler said as if he were speaking to a child.

"Maybe you broke her," Byron said with a sneer.

Blake stopped as he stared at his brother. "What?"

"Oh, hell, Blake, don't get all melodramatic on me. I was just kidding," Byron said, and he tried to look like he didn't care.

But Blake knew his brother cared. That thought somehow made him stop again. He thought back to the last few months, thought of all his times with Jewell, of the good and the bad, of the laughter and tears, the desperation and the peace.

"She does know that you love her, right?" Tyler asked.

"Of course she does," Blake said, but then he stopped again.

Tyler pushed. "Because you've told her."

"Not with words," Blake replied.

"You guys are being ridiculous!" Byron thundered. "Are you listening to what you are saying? Do you want to be just like our father?"

Byron stood up, his chair flying behind him, and both Blake and Tyler watched as he stormed from the room. They sat there a few more moments in stunned silence before Tyler spoke again.

"Don't let this woman get away from you, Blake, or you'll go back to feeling and acting like that," he said as he looked toward the door.

"Byron is fine," Blake insisted. But it was true. He *had* been just like his brother, and not too long ago — not trusting anyone, lying as easily as he spoke the truth, and treating women as nothing more than play toys whose only purpose was to please him.

He didn't want to be that man anymore. He wanted to be the man in love with Jewell. He was the man in love with Jewell. "I haven't said the words, Tyler, but she has to know how much I love her," Blake finally said.

"How can she know if you haven't told her?" Tyler asked.

"Because I show her every single day. We make love and it's burning in my eyes. We snuggle on the couch and I have to touch her. With everything I do, every hour of every single day, I have her in mind. She's my world, her and Justin, and I can't even imagine living without them now," he said.

"Why are you telling *me* this, and not her?" Tyler asked.

"I…I don't know," Blake said. Was he the biggest of fools? It felt like it.

"Look, she's had a rough year, Blake, and even though you were an ass, she still managed to fall in love with you. So you get this great woman, and you find out you have a son, and you get him too, and then you don't tell her he's your son, and you don't tell her how much you love her. What do you think she's thinking right now?"

"I don't know!" Blake said, frustrated beyond all reason.

"She's thinking that she's disposable," Tyler told him.

"How could she possibly think that?"

"If you ever figure out how a woman's mind works, then please enlighten us all," Tyler said, attempting a joke. Blake wasn't in the mood.

"I won't lose her, Tyler. I can't!"

"Then go and fight for her," Tyler told him.

"She refuses to speak to me. How can I fight for her if she won't even talk to me?" he asked, furious that he sounded so weak right now.

"You have to prove to her that you love her," he said, and Blake thought he could do that. "And Blake, it won't be easy, because now she has walls in place. So you'd better have one hell of a plan before you storm the fortress."

When Blake left the office building, he had no idea what he was going to do, but he knew for sure that no matter what it took, he would win her back.

CHAPTER THIRTY-ONE

"BREATHE."

Blake stood outside Jewell's door and wondered how long he'd have to wait. He'd knocked, he wouldn't use the key that was burning a hole in his pocket. That wasn't a way to show her he respected her, loved her.

No, he would wait for her to open the door to him. Since she had a peephole, he thought the wait could be a very long time. So he was shocked when he didn't have to wait long at all.

The door opened, and there she was standing before him. He inhaled deeply when he saw the way she looked, and guilt consumed him because he knew that he was the one to blame for those circles beneath her puffy eyes, and the ashen cheeks.

And yet even though she looked as if she'd lost her world, she was still the most beautiful woman he'd ever seen in his life. And it was because he had no doubt that she loved him, that she would be his forever, because he wouldn't leave until she knew that he loved her too.

"You think I married you so I could gain Justin's trust?" he said, deciding it was best to get straight to the point. He didn't think either of them could handle dancing around the subject right now. It was just too painful.

"Yes, Blake, and I don't blame you for it. I don't know what I would have done in your situation had I found out I had a child I knew I could get my hands on," she told him. Her voice so flat, so sad, ripped him to his very soul.

"And you think that I simply used you to get to him?"

She paused before she looked him in the eyes. "Do you really need to hear this, Blake? Do we really need to discuss this? It's done."

"Do you think I love him?"

She paused again and he could see she was thinking over the past couple of months and thinking about them all being together. Yes, he'd bonded with Justin, more than he'd thought possible, and yes, he loved him, heart and soul.

"Yes, I know you do, Blake. I know you'll take care of him." This time, her voice choked up a little bit. It pained him to not grab her, to not comfort her.

"Then you know I won't lose him, right?" he said and this time her eyes filled with tears, and they slowly dripped down her cheeks.

"Why are you doing this to me? I left," she sobbed.

Before he could change his mind, before he grabbed her and lost all focus of what he was doing, he pulled out a document from his attorney. She didn't take it from him; she just looked at him with a trembling lip and glassy eyes.

"I am handing over to you all my legal rights to Justin, such as they are," he told her, holding the file in front of her.

She looked confused as she looked from the document to him and then back at the document. In her confusion, the tears stopped, thankfully, but the deep sadness on her face didn't in any way disappear.

"I...I don't understand," she finally whispered.

"I love Justin. In the short time I have gotten to know him, I have fallen in love with him," he said, and she gave him a little smile. That's how much she loved her brother — enough that just knowing someone loved him was enough to ward off some of the pain she was going through.

"And to lose him now that I've found him would destroy me, but, Jewell, what I thought I've been telling you for so long is that I love you too. I was telling you by showing you instead of using the words, and I guess that was my downfall. But I was mesmerized by you from the first moment our eyes met, and then something changed within me, something happened I never thought possible. The walls I'd built up around my heart when I was a child suddenly began to crack, and one day I realized they were no longer there. You are the reason I wake up in the morning, the reason I can't wait to come home each evening. You're my reason for being happy. I love you, Jewell. I love you so much that I can't imagine living one more moment without you." Blake wanted desperately to take her in his arms, but he knew he needed to wait.

"But...but our marriage wasn't real. It was for the business deal, and for Justin," she said, looking more and more confused.

"The business deal wasn't real, Jewell. I never had a deal where I had to be married. I just...I'm not good at expressing my feelings. And I wanted to marry you. At first it was because I wanted you to be mine, because I couldn't let you get away, but finally I realized it wasn't about possession; it was because my heart belongs to you. You are my everything. You've made me a better man, and I need you to continue to have faith in me so that we can be a family — you, me and Justin. You know, I'll even beg if you want me to."

When she paused for another long moment, Blake felt doubts begin to creep in. What if she had just had too much? What if it his confession was too little too late? He could lose both her and Justin, and he couldn't even imagine how he would manage to survive that.

But if she needed him to walk away, then for her, he would.

Then her lips turned up just a little, and he saw hope return to her eyes. And she took one tentative step toward him, and then another, and then she was wrapping her arms around him.

And Blake knew that they would be okay. He hadn't the foggiest idea how long the two of them stood there with their arms wrapped around each other — what did it matter, after all? — but when she finally pulled back, the love shining from her sparkling eyes was unmistakable.

"I love you so much," she said, "that I have spent the last few days here wondering how I was going to survive losing you. I told myself that my feelings weren't real, but I knew that wasn't the truth. I knew that to live without you would be to leave a piece of my soul behind. I love you, Blake Knight. You have rescued me from a life of unhappiness, and I only hope I will have the chance to show you each and every day how much you mean to me." Jewell pressed her lips to his and sighed in ecstasy.

Blake was lost in her arms for several moments before he drew back again and looked at her. "I can't believe what a fool I've been, Jewell. Thank you for saving me, for saving us. I know that for the rest of our lives we're going to make the world jealous, because our love will be so blinding," he told her.

"We've both been foolish, Blake, but it doesn't matter anymore. All that matters from this point forward is that we always be honest, and that we continue to love each other through the good and the bad," she said, and she kissed his jaw over and over again.

"I promise you, Jewell, that I'll do my damnedest from here on out to make you know you are loved, worshipped, and appreciated. I want to make you the happiest woman alive."

"Oh, Blake, you already have."

"Let's go home," he said to his wife.

And that's just what they did.

EPILOGUE

MCKENZIE FLIPPED OFF her blankets with an angry shove, thrust her feet into her slippers, and blindly reached for her robe. Then she stomped through her house until she reached the front door. The loud pounding continued unabated. It was what had woken her up and put her in such a terrible mood.

"Go away!" she shouted through the door. She didn't give a damn who was knocking. It was two in the morning, and she was not about to invite the ill-mannered person in.

"I'm not leaving until we talk!" a man shouted right back at her.

She froze, suddenly almost overcome by fear. But no. She was McKenzie Beaumont, dammit, and she didn't frighten easily.

"I'm calling the police," she growled.

"Fine with me. The chief is a personal friend," he said with just enough arrogance that he might be telling the truth.

"Who are you?" she asked, her voice much less angry. Despite her bravado, the fear had returned in spades, and a shiver ran down her spine.

"Byron Knight!" he shouted back.

"Byron?" She opened the small window that would show her who was standing on her doorstep. She was shocked to see that it *was* Byron, Blake Knight's brother, who was standing there. "What in the world are you doing on my doorstep at two in the morning?" she asked.

Then she started to panic. What if something had happened to Blake? Or to Jewell? Without thinking, she unlocked the door and thrust it open. "What's wrong? What's going on?"

Though she'd seen the man only a few times before, he took her open door as an invitation and walked right inside.

"What is wrong?" she asked again, truly beginning to worry.

"I have a question for you, Ms. Beaumont," he said, and that's when she smelled the alcohol and noticed the narrowed eyes. She never should have opened her door. She knew Blake. That didn't mean she knew his brother.

"Just ask your question and then get the hell out of my house," she said, thrusting her shoulders back as she got ready to do battle. She had been to hell and back more than once. There was no way this man was going to intimidate her.

"Just who do you think you are?" he said menacingly.

"I'm sorry, Byron, but you're going to have to be a little bit more specific than that," she said, placing her hands on her hips.

"You think you can mess with people's lives and get

away with it. Well, I'm here to prove you wrong."

McKenzie stumbled back a step when he started stalking her, and then she was up against a wall with his arms caging her in.

"If you touch me, I'll press charges," she warned him.

"Oh, McKenzie, you will soon learn I'm not one of the timid little men you're used to dealing with," he warned.

And then his head descended.

You can find more of Melody Anne's titles at all retailers. Here's an excerpt from

THE BILLIONAIRE WINS THE GAME

PROLOGUE

"IT'S JUST NOT right, Katherine!" Joseph slammed his fist down on the table, making the dinnerware shake. "Those kids just don't listen to us—not one of them. Can't they see that we aren't getting any younger? I should've had grandchildren bouncing on my knees years ago."

Katherine smiled as she listened to her husband complain about his disobedient children. She knew what he said was nothing but empty words. He adored their kids as much as she did. She had to agree with Joseph, though, that a few beautiful women rocking babies would be an excellent addition to the house. She'd always dreamed of the day she'd be holding grandchildren while her table was surrounded by those she loved.

"Now, Joseph. You know if you go meddling again, the boys are going to disown you," Katherine warned.

"If they don't do something about this grandchildren situation, then I'm going to disown them," he growled, though with zero conviction in his voice.

"Since you retired last year, you've had too much time on your hands, Joseph Anderson. The boys have been tossed a lot of responsibility already. Are you sure you want to add more to their plates?" she finished, knowing the answer already.

"The boys are ready for love and marriage. They just need a helping push."

The decision had already been made. He'd have at least one grandchild in his empty mansion before Christmas.

Katherine suppressed her sigh, knowing there was nothing she could say that would change her willful husband's mind. Where did he think their sons acquired that particular trait? Even with their flaws, she couldn't possibly love any of them, including her husband, more than she already did.

"Lucas will be first," Joseph said in his booming voice, startling Katherine out of her reverie. "I've already found him the perfect bride."

Joseph leaned back in his chair with a pleased expression on his face. Finally, he had a project to keep himself occupied—with the prize of grandchildren as his reward. Lucas was in for wild adventures come Monday morning.

Katherine watched the self-satisfied expression on Joseph's face and thought about warning her sons about what was coming. She decided against it because even though she didn't agree with Joseph's meddling, she really did want those grandbabies…

CHAPTER ONE

YOU CAN DO this. Walk in there with confidence. Who cares if this family is worth more than Bill Gates and Donald Trump combined? You were hired for this position, and you need this job. They obviously see something in you, so keep your head held high.

Amy was giving herself a lecture on her long elevator ride up to the twenty-fifth floor of the Anderson Corporation. Her stomach was in knots as she began her journey into the corporate world.

She brushed a few strands of escaped golden hair from her face, more out of nervousness than necessity. She considered herself to be of average looks and tried to downplay the assets she'd been given. She wanted to be respected, not lusted after, like her mother. She had long hair she couldn't find the will to cut off, although when out, she always placed it in an unflattering bun.

She tended to hide her curves from the world. She was well endowed, in what an ex-boyfriend had called "all the right places" and she was self-conscious of the fact. She also didn't like the fact that her green eyes gave away every emotion she was feeling, and that no matter how hard she tried, she couldn't manage to fix it.

She still couldn't believe she'd been hired as executive secretary for Lucas Anderson. Anyone who lived within a thousand-mile radius of Seattle, Washington, knew who the Andersons were. Their corporation had a variety of divisions, which required a large staff. They dealt with everything from construction and farming to high-end corporate takeovers. Although their headquarters was in the U.S., they did business all around the world, and she was excited to be a part of it.

Her job was in the corporate headquarters, working for the fairly new president, Lucas Anderson. All she really knew was he'd taken over his father's position about a year ago.

Though she'd graduated with honors, she was still fresh out of college and felt a little bit overwhelmed at the prospect of working for such a powerful man. She hadn't actually met Lucas, yet, just his father.

She'd originally met Joseph at a college fair toward the end of her senior year at the university. He'd given her his card and told her to call after graduation, telling her he was impressed with her college transcript. She'd called the day after her commencement ceremony, and he'd gotten her in for an interview faster than she'd dared to even hope for.

As she continued the long ascent in the elevator, she let her thoughts drift back to the previous week when she'd interviewed for the job.

Amy took a fortifying breath as she stepped from the

cab, looking up at the huge fortress of a home in front of her. Before she could blink, the yellow car pulled away, leaving her frozen at the bottom of the large cement staircase. There was no turning back now.

She slowly climbed the steps and approached the door, which was big enough to fit a large truck through. It seemed Mr. Anderson liked to do things on a much larger scale than the average person.

She rang the doorbell, though he must know she was already there as he'd opened the gates at the bottom of the driveway.

Within seconds, the door was opened by an older gentleman who, thankfully, was smiling.

"Hello, I'm Amy Harper. I have an appointment with Mr. Anderson."

"Good morning, Ms. Harper. It's a pleasure to meet you. Please follow me to the sitting room, where Mr. Anderson will join you shortly," the man offered.

Amy nodded, then followed his quick steps as he led her through the overwhelming home. She couldn't help but look around as her steps echoed off the walls.

The home screamed luxury, from the gorgeous marble floors to the priceless pieces of artwork adorning the walls. The longer they walked, the more out of place she felt. She couldn't figure out what had ever made her think she could handle such a prestigious job as to work for the head of a multibillion-dollar corporation.

They walked through a set of oversized double doors and Amy looked around the warm room as her shoulders relaxed. A fireplace, so large she could literally walk inside of it, was burning what smelled like cedar, giving the room a comforting quality. Though the room was well lit, it was done in soft bulbs, making the space incredibly inviting.

"Would you like something to drink while you wait?"

Amy shook her head and gave the man a small smile. She didn't want to appear rude.

"Go ahead and make yourself comfortable in the seating area. I'll let Mr. Anderson know you've arrived."

Before Amy could respond, he exited, leaving her standing near the entrance. Eventually she was able to make her feet respond to her brain and walked over to the comfortable-looking sofa. She sank onto the soft leather and leaned back. She wasn't kept waiting long before a rumbling voice startled her, causing her to sit straight up. She was thankful she hadn't accepted the drink or she would've spilled it all over herself.

"Good morning, Ms. Harper. I'm sorry to have kept you waiting. Sometimes it's difficult to get off the phone," Joseph said.

"I haven't been waiting long at all, Mr. Anderson. Thank you for getting me in for an interview so quickly. I really appreciate it." Amy jumped to her feet and moved forward to shake his hand.

"The pleasure's all mine. Now, let's get the formality out of the way. Call me Joseph, please," he said as he held out his hand.

Amy felt like she was caught before an oncoming train. She didn't know how to react. She couldn't be rude, but she was uncomfortable calling him by his first name. She took his hand as she shifted on her feet.

"Thank you. You can call me Amy," she finally replied, deciding to just not call him by any name.

"Now that we have the formalities out of the way, let's sit down and chat. Have you been offered something to drink?"

"Yes, but I don't need anything." She didn't think she'd be able to swallow past the nervous lump in her throat.

Joseph indicated for her to sit back down on the sofa, which she quickly did, grateful to get off her shaky legs. He took the chair opposite her, then trained his light blue eyes on her face. The man was quite intimidating, standing well over six feet tall, with the broadest shoulders she could ever remember seeing.

He had snow white hair, just starting to thin a bit, and a neatly trimmed white mustache and beard. He was actually quite handsome for a man who must be in his early fifties at least.

"I was impressed with your résumé during the job fair at your school. If I remember correctly, you've held regular jobs since you were fourteen, then full-time work all throughout your schooling, correct? How did you manage to regulate your time to keep such impressive grades?"

"I've always believed in a strong work ethic. I made sure not to overschedule myself, and I took my classes a little later in the morning so I could work the swing shifts at my jobs. I didn't want to graduate with a lot of debt," Amy replied, *happy in knowing she'd done exactly that and was pretty much debt free.*

"Very impressive, Amy. Your résumé here, says you graduated with a degree in business finance with a minor in public relations. What are your future plans?"

"I haven't had a lot of time to think about where I want to go in ten years, but my goal has always been to get my foot in the door of a great corporation, such as yours, and work my way up. I know it's not an easy task, but I learn very quickly, and I'm not afraid of hard work or long hours. I'll do whatever it takes to learn all I need to in order to be

a real asset to your company."

"What about marriage and babies?" he asked, never taking his gaze from her eyes.

Amy felt her cheeks heat at his question. She knew a lot of higher-up companies were afraid to hire young women due to the fact they'd sometimes get married, then need time off for having children and such. She didn't want to lie, but she knew her answer could lose her the job.

"I'm not involved with anyone right now, but I'd be lying to you if I said I don't want that to happen. I eventually want children, whether I do so in the traditional way or I adopt. I've always wanted to be a mother, but I can guarantee you I wouldn't let anything affect my job performance. I know the value of secure employment, and I can't be a great mother without first having a solid home for my child," she answered. She knew he didn't know her, but she could obtain letters of recommendation. She'd never once taken a sick day from work, and her school assignments had always been on time, if not early.

Joseph continued watching her for so long, it made her want to fidget in her seat. With sheer will, she remained still as she waited for his response.

"Do you have family or friends close by who'd be willing to help you?"

Amy was surprised by his questions. She'd never before had an interview with so many personal questions. It was throwing her off balance. She had all the answers to typical interview questions, but not the stuff he was asking her. She didn't want anyone to know the true circumstances of her personal life.

"I have a few friends, but no family here," she finally answered, feeling safe in her choice of wording. The reality

was that she didn't have any family, period.

Joseph then switched back to asking a few more work-related questions and she relaxed, secure in her knowledge of the business world. She'd studied hard and spent the very little free time she had researching large corporations, knowing she wanted a high salary job when she graduated.

Her real goals included her working nonstop for several years while saving every extra dime she could so she'd be able to have a family. She'd been alone since she was a child, and she didn't want to die that way.

What Amy didn't know was that Joseph had already run a full background check on her, knew she was an orphan, and he had much bigger ideas in mind than just an executive assistant position. He was looking for a potential daughter-in-law.

"Amy, it's been a true pleasure talking with you today. As you were my last interview, I can safely tell you that the position is yours if you'd like it."

Amy stared back at Joseph in shock. She hadn't expected to hear anything about the job for at least a week and found herself speechless as his words sunk in. He smiled as he waited for her to compose herself.

"Um…thank you, Mr. Anderson. I…Of course, I'll take the job," she finally stuttered, completely forgetting about his request to call him by his first name.

"That's wonderful. Welcome to the Anderson family corporation…"

The elevator sounding her arrival snapped Amy back to the present. *Do not blow this job, Amy. If it all works out, you could be completely secure within a couple years.* With her final words of encouragement to herself, she took a deep breath and waited for the doors to open.

As she stepped onto the twenty-fifth floor, she was momentarily paralyzed with fear. It was the most beautiful office she'd ever seen. The doors opened up to a massive lobby, a round cherry wood desk strategically placed for easy guest access. Behind the desk was a stunning blonde who looked more efficient than Amy ever hoped to be. White marble columns flanked the entranceway, leading to where Amy assumed the offices were located. Exquisite paintings hung on the walls, adding a depth of warm color. In the corner a seating area offered soft leather furniture and an antique coffee table with a priceless chandelier acting as a centerpiece overhead. She felt increasingly frumpy and inadequate as she stepped forward in her second-hand business suit and three-year-old heels.

"Can I help you?" the woman asked.

Amy snapped out of her temporary paralysis and walked forward. "Yes, I'm Amy Harper, the new executive secretary for Mr. Anderson," she said with as much confidence as she could rally.

The woman looked at her blankly for a moment before slowly reaching for her phone. "Mr. Anderson, I have Amy Harper here who says she's your new executive secretary." She paused for a few moments. "Okay…Yes, sir."

She hung up the phone and turned back to Amy, "Mr. Anderson says he already has an executive secretary and has hired no one new. He also said that if you're a reporter trying for another story about his family, all his answers are *no comment*." The woman looked dismissively at Amy before adding, "Have a nice day, Ms. Harper."

She didn't give Amy another glance as she turned back to her computer. As far as she was concerned, Amy was dismissed.

"Um, excuse me," Amy looked at the secretary's nameplate "...Shelly, I was interviewed last week by Mr. Anderson. He told me to be in the office at eight A.M. sharp, so you may want to check again," she said a bit more forcefully. Shelly glanced up, as if shocked that the disturbing woman was still there.

Before Shelly had a chance to reply, the elevator chimed and in walked an older woman with smiling blue eyes. "You must be Amy Harper. I'm sorry I'm late but I got stuck behind a car accident," the woman said while walking forward. "I'm Esther Lyon and I'll be working with you this week getting you trained for the new position. I was so happy when Joseph called to let me know he'd found my replacement," she said, warmth seeping through her voice.

Relief flooded through Amy, knowing the job was really hers, for better or worse. "It's so good to meet you, Esther. I was a bit nervous when Shelly said there wasn't a job," she said.

Esther looked over at the woman in question. "We haven't yet announced I'm retiring, though it's been in the works for some time. Shelly wasn't made aware of the situation. I'm sorry about any lack of communication.

"Walk with me, and I'll show you your new office as I talk a little about the history of this wonderful company. The original building was created a little over one hundred years ago, but in this growing city, many updates have been added since then. Joseph's grandfather, Benjamin, started Anderson Corporation with little more than a prayer and a few dollars. As I'm sure you know, his hard work paid off. We're now global, with offices all across the

United States and the world. Joseph was the next elected CEO after Benjamin's passing, but his son, Lucas, took over last year, and is certainly following in his relative's footsteps. He's a brilliant man, and I'm sure you'll love working for him."

"I have to be honest," Amy said with awe. "This is all a little overwhelming. I mean, the history of this wealthy family, the amount of business to keep track of, even the building itself. I don't know how one man keeps track of it all."

"Oh, it takes a whole team, sweetie, believe me. Don't let yourself get worked up over nothing. The way to keep sane in this chaotic place is simply to do one task at a time. Look at the smaller picture, and before you know it, the day is done and you've accomplished far more than you ever imagined," Esther reassured her.

They walked down the hallway and through a large oak doorway into a huge office. Was everything in the building done on a much grander scale than your average place? In the middle of the room was a huge three-sided desk. On the surface sat a top-of-the-line computer and an overflowing In and Out box. Two chairs were placed in front of the desk and one large chair behind it.

A bookshelf took up most of one wall, its shelves lined from top to bottom with many titles. Amy hoped she wasn't expected to read them all in a short time period. Hopefully, they were only there for either decoration, or for when she needed a specific answer, though with the Internet, it was much faster to search online for whatever a person needed nowadays.

Natural light flooded the room from the floor-to-ceiling windows lined up on the back wall behind the desk.

234 Excerpt from THE BILLIONAIRE WINS THE GAME

Amy was grateful for the uncovered windows, knowing if she got too stressed, she could take a minute to face the amazing city of Seattle while her stress had a chance to diminish. It really was an ideal office.

"Come in and have a seat. Make yourself comfortable while I show you what you need to get started. Before you know it, you'll be excellent on your own, no longer needing my help at all," Esther said kindly.

"I have my doubts about that, but I'm sure glad you're the one training me. You seem very nice."

"Thank you, Amy. Do you mind if I call you by your first name? I've never been huge on the formality thing. I feel that an office environment should be enjoyable, and *really* knowing who you're working with makes a big difference in making it so. Joseph became a dear friend of mine, and so did his beautiful wife, Katherine. I've watched their children grow into fine young men and have been treated like a part of their family. It's a good thing, too, because there are weeks you'll see far more of this office than your own place. You need to have a healthy working relationship with your boss."

"I'd love to keep it informal. Joseph said the same thing to me during the interview, and I didn't know how to respond, but I'm beginning to see this place isn't what I thought it would be. I was expecting a rigid staff and endless work," Amy replied. As she realized what she said, she quickly tried to correct herself.

"I wasn't trying to say hard work is bad, or being professional is a negative thing. I was just…"

"You don't need to explain, Amy," Esther interrupted. "I understand exactly what you're saying. Before I was fortunate enough to get a job with Joseph, I worked for a large developer on the other side of the city. He was rude, to me and his clients, never smiled at anyone, and didn't care about those who worked for him. He only cared about the bottom line. There are a lot of corporations like that, but this isn't one of them. They expect a great deal from you, but they're also willing to compensate you for your work. They treat their staff, from the lowest positions to the highest, with respect. The benefits are almost mind-boggling, but you'll soon learn why they can do this. They save a lot of money by having an incredibly low turnover rate, and they never hurt for more business, because they have repeat business in all their divisions. Even in bad economic times, they not only survive, but thrive."

Amy relaxed as she listened to Esther. The woman should be a recruiter for the corporation, not that it looked as though they needed to recruit. Before that moment, Amy hadn't realized quite how lucky she was to have gotten her job. It didn't matter, though. She'd work hard no matter what; she didn't know any other way.

Amy felt slightly overwhelmed as the two women worked together the rest of the morning. By the afternoon, she was starting to pick up on some of the tasks, though, and she really enjoyed Esther's company. They worked well together, and Amy wished she had more than one week of training with her. Amy didn't have a mother and tended to enjoy the company of older women, especially when they were open and caring.

Esther put Amy on a project as she cleaned out her email. Amy was glad to find she was able to do the assigned task without asking for help. They sat in a comfortable silence as they worked for a few hours before they were interrupted.

"Esther, can you cancel my appointments for the rest of the day. I need to go to my father's. Before I leave, I also need the Niles reports if you've finished them."

Amy looked up as the most stunning man she'd ever glimpsed walked through a connecting door on the south wall. He was looking at a piece of paper in his hand, which gave her a few moments to secretly observe him.

The first thing she noticed was his build. He had to be at least six-foot-four, with wide shoulders, a full chest, and a flat stomach. As his arm moved, stretching the obviously tailored dark business suit, she could easily guess he was solid muscle, not an ounce of fat daring to attach to his body. The white shirt clearly accentuated his golden tan. The outfit was complete with a loosened tie, making him look like he'd just stepped off the closest movie shoot rather than his office.

He reached up and ran his fingers through his dark brown hair, causing the short strands to stick out in a few places, making him even sexier, in her opinion. In the next moment he looked up, and his deep azure eyes met her startled green ones.

"I'm sorry, Esther. I didn't realize you had a client in here."

Amy was shocked by his words. Why was he calling her a client?

"Lucas Anderson," he said as he held his hand out to her. *I'm in trouble, big, big trouble,* was her only thought as she looked at his hand as if it were a snake. Skin-to-skin contact would feel far too intimate, even though it was simply shaking hands, but when had she ever touched a man of this stunning caliber? She also knew full well she couldn't refuse to shake her boss's hand.

As she hesitated an awkward amount of time, she saw him raise his eyebrows at her questioningly. Her face turned a nice shade of red as she finally broke eye contact.

She snapped out of her trance, realizing he was waiting for her to introduce herself. Finally, she stood and gave him her hand. "Hello, I'm Amy Harper."

Amy was rooted to the spot as his fingers closed around hers, her breath instantly held prisoner inside her lungs.

The Billionaire Wins the Game is available at all retailers.